Alfred C Hills

MacPherson

The Confederate Philosopher

Alfred C Hills

MacPherson
The Confederate Philosopher

ISBN/EAN: 9783742818690

Manufactured in Europe, USA, Canada, Australia, Japa

Cover: Foto ©Andreas Hilbeck / pixelio.de

Manufactured and distributed by brebook publishing software
(www.brebook.com)

Alfred C Hills

MacPherson

MACPHERSON,

THE GREAT

CONFEDERATE PHILOSOPHER

AND

SOUTHERN BLOWER.

A RECORD

OF

HIS PHILOSOPHY, HIS CAREER AS A WARRIOR, TRAVELLER,
CLERGYMAN, POET, AND NEWSPAPER PUBLISHER, HIS
DEATH, RESUSCITATION, AND SUBSEQUENT
ELECTION TO THE OFFICE OF

GOVERNOR OF LOUISIANA.

BY

ALFRED C. HILLS,

EDITOR OF THE NEW ORLEANS ERA.

NEW YORK:

PUBLISHED BY JAMES MILLER,

(SUCCESSOR TO C. S. FRANCIS & CO.,)

522 BROADWAY.

MDCCCLXIV.

TO

MAJOR-GENERAL NATHANIEL P. BANKS,

COMMANDER OF THE DEPARTMENT OF THE GULF,

THE SOLDIER AND STATESMAN,

WHO, BY HIS OWN LABOR AND GENIUS, RAISED HIMSELF FROM THE

OBSCURE AND HUMBLE WALKS OF LIFE, TO ADORN SOME OF THE

MOST HONORABLE CIVIL AND MILITARY POSITIONS; AND

WHO, GUIDED BY THE SAME SPIRIT OF UNSUR-

PASSED PERSEVERANCE, PLANTED THE FLAG

OF HIS COUNTRY ON PORT HUDSON,

BORE IT IN TRIUMPH THROUGH

WESTERN LOUISIANA, AND UP THE RIO GRANDE,

This Volume,

BY PERMISSION, IS INSCRIBED,

BY HIS

SINCERE ADMIRER AND GRATEFUL FRIEND,

THE AUTHOR.

PREFACE.

The "Macpherson Letters" were published in the New Orleans Era during the past year. Their unexpected, and, perhaps, undeserved popularity in the Southwest, and a very general desire on the part of the author's friends to see them in a book, are his reasons for publishing them. His observations in New Orleans led him to believe that ridicule was the most potent weapon that could be employed against the absurd opinions and prejudices of that portion of the people of the Southwest who sympathised with the rebellion. He had, at least, the gratification of knowing that they were very generally read, not only in the army and navy, but by the people, many of whom believed, for some time, that "Macpherson" was an actual citizen of Madisonville, and a genuine correspondent of the Era.

The blind prejudices, the profound political ignorance, the strong passions and boundless credulity of the rebels in New Orleans, must appear incredible to those who have always lived in a free community, where freedom of speech is tolerated, and where universal education renders every one more or less familiar with passing events and the topics of the times. But those who have freely mingled with that class of Louisianians who still cling to the faith of Jeff. Davis, will not be surprised to learn that Macpherson's philosophy was so much in accordance with theirs, and that his exaggerated style of speech was so faithful a copy of secession bombast, that the "great Confederate Philosopher" was, for some weeks, quite a favorite with the hot-headed rebels of the Crescent City.

Many of the incidents which the author attempted to ridicule in these "Letters," were too local in their character to be understood by a reader not familiar with the facts. So far as practicable, these parts have been omitted in this publication, and such explanatory notes have been prefixed to each chapter, as seemed necessary to give the general reader an understanding of its import.

The author will state that when he commenced the publication of these letters, he had no expectation of writing but one; and to that he signed the first name that occurred to him, without reflection. He was not then aware that an officer named James B. McPherson held a commission in the United States Army,—an ignorance due, probably, to the fact that for many months the author was in service where newspapers seldom reached him. But the officer in question, by his gallant conduct on many hard-fought fields, has made a national reputation for skilful and daring generalship, and his name is as familiar as household words to all who have read the story of Vicksburg, and of the various movements of the noble army of General Grant.

A. C. H.

NEW ORLEANS, LA., *January*, 1864.

CONTENTS.

CHAPTER I.

PAGE

Free Trade with the Rebels...................................... 13

CHAPTER II.

Mr. Macpherson hath Hopes for his Idiotic Boy.—He declareth himself to be a good Union Man.—Correspondence, and the Way to send it.—The True Plan of Conciliation, etc......... 16

CHAPTER III

The Great Secession Demonstration in New Orleans, as described by Louis T. Wigfall Macpherson.......................... 19

CHAPTER IV.

Macpherson takes the Oath of Allegiance.—A Letter from Jeff. Davis.—A Good Confederate Lady with Yankee Boarders.— A Gross Insult to the Confederacy, etc., etc................. 25

CHAPTER V.

Macpherson, Journeying to Madisonville, sees the Great Confederate Cross in the Heavens.—He is seized by Arizonian Guerillas, and taken to the Place of Execution.—His Escape from Death, etc.. 34

CHAPTER VI

A Full Account of the Great Macpherson Festival at the House of the Noble Woman, in New Orleans..................... 45

1*

CHAPTER VII.

PAGE

Mac Pherson setting up as a Confederate Planter, &c.—explains
the Destination of Race to his Native Zouaves—A great history
and Adventures of the Culinary Cass—Macpherson captured
by Darwin's Zouaves.—Interview with the "Southern Search,"
&c., &c. 55

CHAPTER VIII.

The Great Charity Fair...................................... 66

CHAPTER IX.

The Confederate Arithmetic................................. 81

CHAPTER X.

Hymn of Salvation... 84

CHAPTER XI.

Macpherson dedicates himself to War and Larceny.—He encounters the Honest Jew....................................... 85

CHAPTER XII.

The Great Confederate Traveller describes his Journey through
the Louisiana Lowlands Low................................ 91

CHAPTER XIII.

Macpherson appears as a Clergyman, and expounds the Confederate Gospel.—He encounters the Weeping Orphan, and unexpectedly finds a Large Family on his hands.—He preaches
from the Text : "Blow ye!" etc., etc...................... 103

CHAPTER XIV.

Macpherson as a Military Chieftain.—He is appointed a Major
General of Confederate Volunteers.—He issues a Proclamation,
raises an Army, and wins two Battles in a single Day, etc., etc. 118

CHAPTER XV.

PAGE

Macpherson encounters and shoots a Midnight Assassin.—He conscripts Negroes, and addresses them In a manner calculated to arouse their Zeal in the Confederate Cause.—He appoints his Staff, etc., etc.................................. 125

CHAPTER XVI. *

The Registered Enemies of the United States leave the Department of the Gulf.—General Macpherson superintends their Departure.—He "Gobbles" them as soon as they arrive in his Dominions.—He unexpectedly meets the Honest Jew, etc., etc. 182

CHAPTER XVII.

An Account of the Death of James D. Macpherson, the Great Confederate Philosopher, Warrior, Author, and Southern Blower.. 142

CHAPTER XVIII.

The Resuscitation of Macpherson.—It is Discovered that he was not Dead, only Dead Drunk.—His Method of Paying Debts.—He makes the Acquaintance of the Reliable Gentleman, etc., etc... 140

CHAPTER XIX.

Macpherson encounters the Cussed Fool of Carondelet street.—Betting on Vicksburg and Port Hudson.—Fourth of July Celebration at Madisonville, etc., etc. 160

CHAPTER XX.

The Phantom Confederate; or, the Ghost of Madisonville. (A True Story)... 163

CHAPTER XXI.

Macpherson is arrested for Assault and Battery.—He expounds the Law of Responsibility.—He visits Port Hudson and Vicksburg.—He tests the Homœopathic Principle, and is Chased by the Devil, etc., etc.................................... 175

CHAPTER XXII.

PAGE

Macpherson is seized with the Newspaper Mania, and Determines
to become an Editor.—He dissolves the Army of Madisonville,
etc., etc.. 183

CHAPTER XXIII.

Macpherson, disgusted with the Newspaper Business, resolves
to acquire Office and Civil Renown.—The Restoration of Civil
Government in Louisiana.—Macpherson is elected Governor
of the State, etc., etc.................................... 188

CHAPTER XXIV.

The Governor is besieged by Office-seekers.—The Ingenious
Method by which he dispersed the Mob.—The True Southern
Patriot, and why he would not accept Office.—The Idiotic Boy
chastised.—The Governor makes a Pilgrimage to Richmond.—
The Full and Authentic History of the Congressional Career
of the Cussed Fool and the Solitary Horseman, etc., etc...... 199

THE LETTERS

OF

JAMES B. MACPHERSON.

———◆———

CHAPTER I.

FREE TRADE WITH THE REBELS.

NOTE.—Madisonville is a town situated on the Tchefuncta river, near Lake Pontchartrain, and was within the rebel lines at the time these letters were written, as it is, in fact, at the present time. The people were known to be destitute of many of the necessaries of life, and the secessionists of New Orleans made a strong effort to induce the authorities to permit free trade across the lake, on the ground that humanity required it, and that the people were non-combatants. The *Daily Picayune* advocated this theory, and a writer, signing himself "Observer," published a communication in that paper urging its adoption by the authorities. The notion appeared too absurd to be treated seriously, and the author attempted to exhibit it in this light in the following letter, which appeared in THE ERA, February 17th, 1863.

MADISONVILLE, LA.,
Sunday Evening, February 15.

SIR:—I have a wife and twelve children, all of them sons except the wife. Nine of them are in the Confederate service, and so am I. The other three are not in the service, because one of them is only three years old, but he will probably be old enough to join the army before the United States are crushed. Another one has lost a leg in the war, so that he can't march; and the other one is idiotic. I am home on a furlough, and find my wife and three sons bad enough off. They are destitute of many of the necessaries of life, and for my part I don't know what they will do.

I think the United States ought to supply them with food. They are non-combatants, and there is no chance that any of them will ever fight except the youngest; and stipulation might be made that he should not eat any of the food sent over, if that should be deemed necessary.

So long as I and the nine able bodied boys stay in the Confederate army, it will be necessary to have the rest of the family receive supplies from New Orleans; and humanity and philanthropy demand that trade should be allowed.

I was pleased to read in this morning's *Picayune*, a communication from Mr. Observer, on this point. He proposes to send salt and other indispensable articles, and says he would go into the business himself, if he had the means, and could get the necessary authority. I hope he will go into it at once, as we need the salt much, and the indispensable articles would also come handy. He can make a good thing of it, as we are willing to pay a large price for salt, flour, quinine, clothing, cotton-cards, etc., all of which will bring a larger price here than Observer will have to give for them in New Orleans. I would pay a large price for what my family needs, as I could fight a great deal better if I knew the folks were comfortable at home.

By all means let some one lend Mr. Observer the capital if he hasn't got it, for there is no reason why non-combatants shouldn't be fed.

Yours, sincerely,

JAMES B. MACPHERSON.

P. S.—While you are about it, tell Observer to bring me an English rifle, with a cartridge-box, and a hundred rounds of ammunition.

J. B. M.

CHAPTER II.

Mr. Macpherson hath Hopes for his Idiotic Boy.—He declareth himself to be a good Union Man.—Correspondence, and the Way to send it.—The True Plan of Conciliation, etc.

Note.—Confederate prisoners who were to leave New Orleans on parole, were discovered to have contraband letters sewed into their clothing.

MADISONVILLE, LA.,
February 21st, 1863.

Sir:—I find that THE ERA published my letter, in which I showed that the United States ought to support my family as long as I am in the Confederate service, and that the destitute people on this side of the lake should be permitted to trade with New Orleans. When I saw that letter in THE ERA, I experienced all the pleasure of a man who, for the first time, sees his name in print. I looked at it two or three hours, and then handed it over to my Idiotic Boy.

I could not restrain my tears, when I thought of the unhappy fate of that youth, doomed never to write a letter for the newspapers, nor to realize the blissful feelings which swelled in his father's heart, at gazing upon his own name in small-cap letters.

"Cheer up, my dear," said my wife. "James, to be sure, is an idiot, but idiots does sometimes write for newspapers."

Immediately she handed me "Observer's" letter in Sunday's *Picayune*, and I became calm. Whenever I look at that letter I believe fully my wife's remark.

As I told you before, I am home on a furlough, and so long as I remain away from my regiment, at Port Hudson, I consider myself a non-combatant, and I demand from the United States government all the rights of a neutral. I wish, while my furlough continues, to take a hand in trade across the lake, and as Observer promises to go into it if anybody will furnish funds, I now definitely offer him my assistance, and promise to invest my last three months' pay as a private, which I have just drawn from the paymaster in Confederate treasury notes and Madisonville butchers' tickets, and three dollars of which are worth three cents in coin.

What I want now, is, to make arrangements for getting all the newspapers across the lake, and to gain information in regard to the Union soldiers in General Banks's Department. So long as I am a neutral, I have a perfect right to know what is going on, and the information thus obtained I could sell to my General for a high price, which would do much towards feeding my destitute family, and helping on our speculations. You will therefore please forward to me immediately a full statement of the number of troops in the Department of the Gulf, where the camps are located, the quality of arms, the number of guns, the amount of ammunition, the number, strength, and position of the gunboats, the maps and plans of future operations by land and water, and any other small matters which would be of interest and use to me, and which can do no harm so long as I am a non-combatant. If, however, the military authorities should differ from the *Picayune* and me in these matters, please sew all necessary letters into the collars and cuffs of the coats of Confederate soldiers, bound only by a *parole* of honor, and stuff all the newspapers you can find into the legs of their breeches.

But there can be no possible objection to permitting free correspondence with *me*. I am, in fact, a good Union man, and boldly proclaim my Union sentiments among my comrades. My doctrine is, that the United States ought to lay down their arms at once, and then ask for an armistice, preparatory to a recognition of the Southern Confederacy. Such a step would place the Confederate States under great obligations to the United States, and would engender a sentiment of friendship. It would, to be sure, result in the complete success of the Confederate cause; but it would heal all feelings of wounded pride on our part, and perhaps ultimately restore the Union. I, for one, would then go for a re-establishment of the Union, on condition that all the Northern men who do not agree with me should be hung or expelled from the country. If the United States would consent to this, and purge itself effectually of all men of opposite politics, I think we might be reunited and live together in peace. But so long as any one favorable to the United States government is tolerated in the North, I, for one, am opposed to the Union, and will urge the Confederate army to fight, and make all I can out of it. Let the United States government pursue a conciliatory policy and hang all its friends, however, and I believe then a happy peace will dawn upon this land, and the advocates of war will skulk away in terror and disgrace.

Yours, truly,

JAMES B. MACPHERSON.

CHAPTER III.

THE GREAT SECESSION DEMONSTRATION IN NEW ORLEANS, AS DESCRIBED BY LOUIS T. WIGFALL MACPHERSON.

NOTE.—On the 20th February, 1863, a large number of rebel prisoners left New Orleans to be exchanged. They were to have been taken on the steamer Empire Parish; but that vessel met with some accident before she got off. The departure of these prisoners was made the occasion of a grand demonstration on the part of the secession women of the city, who thronged the levee by thousands, to express their sympathy for the cause of treason. The prisoners all went away with new suits of clothes, furnished by rebel women in the city, and would have carried other suits had the authorities permitted it. The assembly became so noisy and insolent, that a regiment of soldiers finally cleared the levee.

MADISONVILLE, LA.,
February 28th, 1863.

SIR:—I now forward a copy of the letter of my son Louis T. Wigfall, of the Confederate Army; and here I deem it proper to state that I am a descendant of revolutionary sires, and consequently that I named my sons after the greatest lights of American history. They are: George Washington, Louis T. Wigfall, Thomas Jefferson, Roger A. Pryor, Ben. Wood, John C. Breckinridge, Andrew Jackson, Toussaint l'Ouverture, and Horatio Seymour. Those are the names of my nine boys in the army. The idiot I have named James Buchanan Floyd, the cripple Braxton Bragg, and the infant Mason Slidell. Having promised thus much, I will proceed with the letter:

Louis T. Wigfall Macpherson's Adventures in New Orleans.

Louis T. Wigfall Macpherson writes:

"I've had the biggest kind of a time sense you hurd from Me last. I was took prisoner by the Yanks. I had sworn never to surrender alive, and I never would have done it, only My back happened to be turned at the minit, and so they got Me and sent Me to New Orleans with the rest. They locked me up for a while, but then they let Me out on payroll in the streets, and I had the fredum of the sitty.

"Well, as I went saunchering along the streets I met a lady whose dress and proud bearing told me at once she belonged to the alight, and so it proved. She stopped and looked at me inquiringly, and finally bending her proud head towards me, she says: 'Pardon Me, sir, but isn't you a Confederate soljur?' Says I: 'Yes, miss, I is.' Says she to Me: 'I thought so by your proud and hauty bearing, and by your dilapidated gray garments, which is dearer in my eyes than the vestments of a monarch, or the costly robes of the Prince de Joinville.' Then I bent my hauty head towards her and said: 'I thank you, miss; you do Me proud.' Then says she: 'Come and see us;' and says I: 'Where do you live;' Then she told me, and I went to see 'em that very night.

"I found that the family belonged to the alight, and was all of the wright stripe. The lady had ate dauters, seven of them grown up, and all of them lovely and charming as rose-blossoms, and all as seccsh as Lovell or Vallandigham. The old lady had a stick about two feet long, which she had saved from the rebel flagstaff at Fort Jackson ever since our victory there over Farrigut. It was beautiful to see her wave this stick over the heads of her obedjunt dauters and hurrah for the Confederacy.

"Says all of them to Me : 'Make this your home as long as you are in New Orleans.' Says I : 'Thank you, kind ladies, I will do so ;' and I did. I staid in that house until I was exchanged, and it was beautiful and romantic to see the devotion of them lovely dauters of the South. I was as ragged as Lazarus, and hadn't a red, and so the old lady sent for a Confederate taylor, and had him make Me a sute of close—a nice gray uniform ; and then they took Me up to the photographic gallery and had My likeness took. But this wouldn't do, and each of the ate dauters had a sute made, and each one of them presented me with a Confederate uniform complete.

" Purty soon the time cum to be exchanged on the Empire Parish, and then I put on my whole nine sutes at a time. I felt grand and looked like the Irysh jiunt, only not as tall. Says they all : 'We are sorry to lose your society, but the Confederacy needs your services, and we must let you go.' Then they all cryed.

"It was now time to go down to the boat, and these lovely ladies was determined to show their devotion to our hoely cawse. So the old lady took her stick, and she with the ate dauters, all wearing seceshun flags around their wastes, formed a holler square around Me, and I marched in the senter with them as a escort of onur. As we was going to the levee we met a Yank soljur, who shouted out : 'Go it, grayback !—you need

an escort of women.' The old lady said: 'I'll take no
insult from a Yank!' and then she knocked him down
with the peace of the flag-staff allowded to; and I ap-
plawded her and the dauters laft. It was a beautiful
site to behold that woman bend her proud and hauty
head and raise her delicate white snowy arm in the
cawse of her country, and to see those lovely dauters,
so alight, smiling sweetly upon her.

"There was a glorious time at the Levee. Holler
squares kept coming in, and all true to the cawse; and
in order to show em I was not afrade to fite, I knocked
a big nigger off the wharf into the river. Just as I
was going a board, the old lady slapped Me on the
shoulder; but I didn't feel it, her hand was so delicate
and I had so many sutes of gray close on. But says
she: 'There's one thing I've forgot.' Then she ripped
open my cuffs and collers, and sode in a catalogue of
Farragut's ships and General Banks's troops, saying:
'That's for Jeff. Davis.' Says I: 'Miss, I'm on my
payroll of onur not to do so.' Says she: 'A Confederate payroll is not wuth a red,' or words to that effect;
and so after they had put a newspaper and a plug of
tobacker in each pocket, they all kissed Me, and the old
lady said: 'Bravo son of the Confederacy!—the alight
of the city has come to see you off and to shour on your
heads the blessings of patryotic matruns and spotless
mades, and to fill your pockets with letters and tobacker. Axcept these toakuns of our patryotic devo-
shun, and think of us when you are far above Baton
Rouge!' Says I: 'Thanks, miss, to you and your ate
alight dauters for your patryotic wishes, for the tobacker
you have bestowed on my unworthy head, and for

teaching me the value of a Confederate payroll of onur.'

" Then I went aboard, and the old lady she swung her stick and we all give three cheers for Jeff. Davis; and then I fell off of the paddle-box into the river, over-cum with the manly emotions which swelled in my bosom. A Yank pulled me out, for I had so many close on I couldn't stur. If I ever meet him in battle I'll ring his neck for him.

" I was so heavy with wet close and things that it took the whole ship's crew to pull me out. They set me on the paddle-box, and I was so heavy that the whole concern broke down, and they had to put us on another ship.

" As soon as we got up to Port Hudson, I sold all my close for $800 a sute, bringing me a total of $7,200, and now I'm perfectly destitute—haven't got a decent sute to put on. Send my order to the United States for a new uniform, and invest my money in salt and ship it up to Port Hudson on a flag-of-truce-boat im-mediately, and oblige

" Your destitute son,

" LOUIS T. WIGFALL MACPHERSON,

" Co. I, 18th La. Vols."

Mr. Macpherson's Views on Negro Soldiers.

I now wish to make a few remarks on the subject of negro soldiers. I am opposed to negroes in the abstract, and am dead set against having them enlisted as soldiers in the service of the United States; and I regard such enlistments as inhuman, wicked, barbarous, and damna-ble beyond description. The English Dictionary does not contain adjectives strong enough to paint the horrors of making Union soldiers of negroes; but when you come to make them Confederate soldiers, I, for one, am in favor of it; and if nine regiments are raised, I mean that each of my sons shall be a Colonel. I will then get my furlough cancelled, and take the field in person, as a Brigadier-General, in command of the Macpherson Brigade. As soon as the war is over I will buy a plantation and set them at work on it, and I mean to be the largest slaveholder and autocrat in the Confederacy.

Yours respectfully,

JAMES B. MACPHERSON.

CHAPTER IV.

MACPHERSON TAKES THE OATH OF ALLEGIANCE.—A LETTER
FROM JEFF. DAVIS.—A GOOD CONFEDERATE LADY WITH
YANKEE BOARDERS.—A GROSS INSULT TO THE CONFEDER-
ACY, ETC., ETC.

NOTE.—Many secessionists in New Orleans took the oath of allegiance to the United States, merely to save their property from confiscation. It was not uncommon for them to boast that such was
their *only* motive, and that they did not regard the oath as binding
upon their consciences. This was true of some who gained their
daily bread by boarding Federal officers. It was not an unusual
spectacle to see ladies cross the street rather than pass under a flag
of the United States; this was one way in which they exhibited
their hatred of the Union, and their sympathy for the rebel cause.

MADISONVILLE, LA.,
March 7th, 1863.

SIR:—You should know that my letters in THE ERA
have been regularly forwarded to Jeff. Davis, at Richmond. With the one in last Sunday's paper, I sent a
request that my furlough might be extended; and in
reply I received, by telegraph, the following:

Letter from Jeff. Davis.

"RICHMOND, VA., March 8.

"MY DEAR MACPHERSON:—I have received from
time to time the copies of THE ERA containing your
wise and patriotic letters, which I have read with ever-
increasing pleasure. The sufferings of your family and
the destitution which prevails among my subjects have
touched my paternal heart; and I now recommend
that you go at once to New Orleans and take the oath

2

of allegiance. Of course you will understand that no oath is binding upon the conscience of a Confederate, unless taken before a Confederate magistrate. Having eaten enough to last you until your next visit, and made such observations as will be useful to the cause, you will return on the first flag-of-truce-boat, and immediately communicate to me all information you can obtain. Also, bring your satchel full of edibles for your family.

"I have directed my Adjutant-general, S. Cooper, to make out a new furlough for you, excusing you from all duty with your regiment, so long as you continue to write for THE ERA.

"I also forward herewith a commission for your son, John C. Breckinridge Macpherson, as Colonel of the 8th Georgia Negro Confederate Liberty Guards.

"I am, my dear Mac,

"Yours in Confederate bonds,

"JEFF. DAVIS."

I was proud enough, the Lord knows, when I first saw my name printed in THE ERA; but what shall I say of my feelings when I received the above letter? "Is it possible," I cried aloud, clasping my hands and raising my eyes impressively, in a manner which would do credit to Vining Bowers; "is it possible that the President of the new nation, the anchor of Southern independence, the flag-staff of our proud stars and bars, the chiefest demigod of Confederate mythology, has condescended to write to me in terms of fraternal endearment?" I clasped my Idiotic Boy to my bosom, waved my letter aloft to heaven, seized my satchel,

and, with emotions only equalled by those of Floyd when he first espied the United States treasury building, started hurriedly for New Orleans.

Macpherson's manly Struggle with his Conscience.

The first encounter I had was with my own conscience. Said conscience to me: "Macpherson, remember that thou art the descendant of revolutionary sires, the proud representative of an honorable house and name, the great light and mirror of Madisonville chivalry, and, more than all, the confidential agent of Jeff. Davis, the greatest man that ever trod in Confederate shoes, worth $300 a pair. Then how canst thou, O Macpherson, lover of honor and hater of Yankees, raise thy hand to heaven and swear allegiance to a flag which, to thine illuminated mind, is the symbol of ungodly power and basest tyranny? and how canst thou consent to eat the bread of Yankees, gotten under the false pretense that thou art faithful to their flag? O Macpherson! pause and go home!"

But I told my conscience to dry up. Did not Daniel eat the bread of the pagan king, and was not Daniel bold as a lion? "I will take the oath," said I, "but there is not Spaulding's glue enough among living men to stick me to it!"

Macpherson takes the Oath of Allegiance.

Well, I went and took the oath. It was a matter of compulsion. because it was the only way I could get inside the lines without becoming a prisoner; and when a man takes an oath under compulsion, he is allowed to

break it the first chance. But when I went up to take
the oath of allegiance, I asked the Yankee officer if he
would have the goodness to let me look at the Bible
before I swore. He kindly assented, and looking at
the imprint I found it had been published in Boston,
and was a regular abolition concern; and then conscience gave way, and said I could swear to any thing
I chose on a Bible printed north of Mason and Dixon's
line. I swore to a lot of stuff—more than I like to
think of now; but one of the points was that I would
never bear arms against the United States. But to
this I mentally added the words, "so long as my furlough lasts," and my conscience went to sleep as sound-
ly as though it had been soothed by twenty whisky-
skins at Marble Hall.

Macpherson finds a good Confederate Lady.

As I expected to remain in town most of the week,
I resolved to find a boarding-house with some good
Confederate who had taken the oath of allegiance. I
soon discovered such a place—a house kept by a Confederate lady, whose husband and three sons are in our
army, boldly fighting for Southern independence, and
who has taken the oath of allegiance to save the property from confiscation. I found this good lady to be
true blue. "Macpherson," said she, when I applied
for board, "have you taken the oath of allegiance to
the Abolitionists?" I blushed all over, from the crown
of my Confederate head to the soles of my Confederate
shoes, as I replied, "Yes." "Well, then," said this
brave lady, "if you have done that git out of this
house! Them as leaves the army when they ought to

be bearing the burden and heat of the Confederate day, musn't come sneaking around this house for shelter. If I was a man, do you think I would be here? No sir-ee. I would have a Jeff. Davis musket on my shoulder, and would be sending death and blood abroad among the Yankees as a besom of destruction. Where is my sons and husband? Isn't they doing their duty to the Confederacy on the bloody field, and one of them in the commissary department! Oh! I hate cowards and traitors, and a man as leaves the Confederacy and comes over to live on Yankee bread is all three combined in one mean hateful critter, who can't find no encouragement nor shelter under this roof! Git out of here, James B. Macpherson!—or I'll have my nigger kick you into the gutter!"

As she gave utterance to these noble and patriotic sentiments, her tall form was erect, her eyes flashed with Confederate fire like the bolts of Olympian Jove; her fists were clenched in the very ecstasy of anger, and cowering before her for mercy, I could but feel that I was in the presence of a goddess.

"Minerva of Louisiana!" I exclaimed, kneeling before her—"Pallas Athené of the Confederacy! let me explain to you the manner and meaning of my visit. Allow me to—"

Just at this stage of my address, the good lady's nigger, in obedience to a wave of her hand, came stealthily behind me, opened the door, and seizing me by the collar, kicked me out of the house, landing me square in the gutter.

I sat there a considerable time, when suddenly a Yankee officer approached, and he asked me into his

room. To my astonishment, he walked into the very
house from which I had just been so summarily ejected.
I sat down and wrote an explanation of my position,
and sent it to the good lady. In five minutes she sent
for me, said she was delighted to see me, proud to have
me under her roof, and that I needn't pay a picayune
for board as long as I staid there. She then had the
nigger whipped for kicking me out, and from that moment we were fast friends.

I found that her house was full of Yankee officers,
except two beautiful young ladies who boarded there,
and were true as steel to the Confederacy.

"How comes it, madam," I inquired, "that a woman
of your proud and patriotic spirit ever consented to
take the oath of allegiance, or to have your establishment supported by Yankee officers?"

"Because," replied the good lady, "necessity is the
mother of invention, and being a mother myself I can
appreciate it. As to taking the oath of allegiance, that
don't amount to nothing. The oath never went
through my teeth; it was necessary to save my property, and I say it boldly, I have no more respect for that
oath than I have for the President of Hayti. As to
the Yankee boarders, the times has been when there
wasn't Confederate treasury notes enough in Jacob
Barker's safe to hire me to feed a Yankee officer; but
times has changed, and finding that I could live on
Yankees and hate 'em at the same time, I yielded to
the mother of invention."

If Mrs. Macpherson could have looked into my heart,
as the good lady gave utterance to the above honorable
and patriotic sentiments, I fear she might have been

jealous of the lively admiration with which the good lady inspired me. But whatever emotions were rising in my heart were suddenly overwhelmed by a great event.

The two young ladies referred to previously, came into the room, trembling with excitement and pale with ghastly anger.

"Has it come to this!" cried the beautiful maiden. "Are we to be insulted at our very doors!"

My chivalric Madisonville blood was aroused by the sight of suffering beauty. "Haste me to know it!" I cried, springing to my feet, "that I, with wings as swift as meditation or the thoughts of love, may have the vile ruffian whipped. Where is the big nigger that kicked me out of doors? Madam, bring him hither, that we may avenge the injuries of your house!"

"Such insolence!" cried the beautiful maiden, "and at our very door! I never!" and she stamped her delicate foot upon the carpet, as though she would crush the United States beneath it.

"What's the matter?" demanded the good lady, in tones of angelic thunder.

But the beautiful maiden could not answer. She became speechless with patriotic rage, and fell to the earth, pointing to the door and gasping with her fainting breath—

"The flag!—the flag!"

Hastening to the door, we behold a loathsome spectacle. The man living near our door, a citizen of New Orleans, had displayed a United States flag from his dwelling. A more gross insult to the Confederacy and to the good people who have taken the oath of allegiance to save their property, could not be imagined. As the good lady gazed upon that detestable emblem of tyranny and bloody despotism, to which she had taken the oath of allegiance, she ground her teeth together, so that you could hear them around the corner. Then we shut the door, and all fainted.

As soon as we recovered, we held a family consultation, and it was discussed whether to leave for the Confederacy or to commit suicide. The beautiful maiden argued in favor of the latter course, as a sentimental way of serving the Confederacy. "How romantic!" she exclaimed; "what a splendid subject for a Confederate Sylvanus Cobb!—what a touching picture for the artist of *Harper's Weekly* or *Frank Leslie's Illustrated!*—Oh! let us commit suicide, and be first in the book of Confederate martyrs, as a lovely matron and maid, who died rather than live under the flag to which they had taken the oath of allegiance, to save their property! I wish," she added with a sigh, which moved me to tears, "that the whole Southern Confederacy would commit suicide!"

This noble and patriotic sentiment would have prevailed, only we wished to preserve the property and make some more money out of the Yankees; and so we decided that every time we went out of the house, we would go bolt across the street and walk on the other side until we had passed the hateful flag, and then recross the street, thus omitting to walk under it. And the ladies went and took down the name and number of the man who had committed this outrage against the Confederacy, and I immediately sent the memorandum on to Jeff. Davis, asking his protection.

Just before, leaving New Orleans, I got very drunk. In that state I went to the telegraph office and got Bulkley to send the following dispatch to Jeff. Davis:

"DEAR JAVIS:—Honor report drunkenness alarming extent. Banks's army thoroughly demented—18 divisions actual mutiny manifestations increasing Indies true great want of Madisonville bread and whisky. Full particulars in full letters by next dispatch. Blockade broken und Federal fleet sunk.   MAC.

I fear the head of the new nation can't comprehend the above, but it is less obscure than the Southern Confederacy, and he professes to understand that.

Yours untiringly,
JAMES B. MACPHERSON.

P. S.—My Idiotic Boy is preparing an attack on the Know Nothings and Pilgrim Fathers, which will be sent to the *True Delta* for publication.
J. B. M.

2*

CHAPTER V.

MACPHERSON, JOURNEYING TO MADISONVILLE, SEES THE GREAT
CONFEDERATE CROSS IN THE HEAVENS.—HE IS SEIZED BY
ARIZONIAN GUERILLAS, AND TAKEN TO THE PLACE OF EX-
ECUTION.—HIS ESCAPE FROM DEATH, ETC.

NOTE.—The New Orleans *Picayune*, of March 7th, contained the
following extraordinary announcement of a great phenomenon in
the heavens :

A CROSS IN THE HEAVENS.—A well-defined cross was seen in the
sky over Kingston, N. C., some two weeks since. A correspondent,
writing from that point to the Wilmington (N. C.) *Journal*, gives the
following description of the phenomenon :

"The moon rose cloudless. At a little before seven o'clock, two
bright spots, some twelve degrees (Qr. in extent ?) were visible, one
North and the other South, and immediately thereafter a cross was
seen in the heavens, the moon joining the four arms of the cross.
About half-past eight o'clock the Northern light went out, but the
cross and the spot to the South remained until past ten, when I retired.- Can any one tell when the cross appeared before since the
days of Constantine, when the letters of I. H. S. accompanied the
sign ?"

Sibley, it is known, commanded a body of Arizonian cavalry ; and
a detachment of these wild and irregular troops one day "gobbled"
a correspondent of THE ERA. He was made to follow them nineteen
hours, when he was released in consideration of his gold watch and
fifty dollars. The Memphis *Appeal* was in high favor with the secessionists of New Orleans, and its reports of rebel successes were about
as truthful as the account contained in Macpherson's letter. The
guerillas were much given to destroying the telegraph within our
lines.

MADISONVILLE, LA.,
February 14th, 1863.

SIR :—I approach my subject with awe and supersti-
tion.

I am the illuminated Confederate who saw the Great
Cross in the Heavens, described by the Wilmington

Journal, and reverently believed by the New Orleans *Picayune*.

It will be remembered that, on the occasion of my recent visit to New Orleans, where I took the oath of allegiance to the United States, in order to get something to eat, I left that city in a state of beastly intoxication. In one pocket of my breeches I had a bottle of whisky, and in the other a copy of the *Picayune*, of the 7th inst.

As I crossed the line and set foot upon the sacred soil of my beloved Confederacy, I cried aloud : " Hail, sweet Confederacy!—land of my ancestors!—land for which George Washington was shot at by an Indian seventeen times, in a single battle !—for which Jackson fought at New Orleans—for which Burgoyne surrendered at Saratoga Springs, as thousands have done since !—welcome thy faithful Macpherson once more to thy Confederate bosom! What graphic recollections of hunger and thirst crowd upon my patriotic mind, as I tread again thy consecrated soil with a new pair of shoes! For thy sake, I see Ethan Allen demanding the surrender of Ticonderoga, Columbus prowling around in search of the New World, and the Pilgrim Fathers building huts in the wilds of New England !"

Narrow Escape from Death.

Just at this stage of my apostrophe, I was startled by a loud crash, and a flashing line of fire from the thicket in my rear, followed by a voice which cried : " Die, base Yankee dog!" The Confederate picket had been deceived by my allusion to the Pilgrim

Fathers and New England, and, supposing I was a Yankee, had fired upon me a whole volley of Confederate musketry. Overcome by a strong emotion of fear, I fell prostrate upon the soil, and was left for dead. But gathering myself up, I soon discovered that I was as alive as ever, and that the only result of the volley had been to deprive me of a considerable portion of my pantaloons.

Grateful for my deliverance from premature and unnatural homicide, I fell into a train of serious reflection; and conscience, with a heavy hand, chastised me for approaching my native land in a state of beastly intoxication. I therefore fell upon my knees, and took the pledge of perpetual temperance. I vowed in the most solemn manner that never again, while life should last or the Confederacy endure, would I, under any circumstances, taste, touch, or handle one drop of spirituous or malt liquors, wine, Louisiana rum, or cider. I then danced a double-shuffle, and chanted the *Bonnie Blue Flag*, with a snatch of *Stonewall Jackson's Grand March.*

Overcome by patriotic emotions, I determined to modify my temperance pledge so far as to take one big swig of whisky. And as I had now come within sight of Madisonville, I sat down by the fence, and taking the bottle from my pocket, cried aloud: "O Bacchus! son of Jupiter and Semelé, thou the victim of Juno's unrelenting hatred, who didst cause the women of Thebes to run wildly through the woods like Confederate Gorillas, to thee I dedicate my last parting drink!" I then took the biggest swig of whisky I ever took in my life, and the effect was so pleasing, that I kept drinking until the bottle was empty.

The Vision.

In this frame of mind, and while still seated by the highway, under the fence, I imagined myself at home in my own room. I trust I shall be excused for alluding to the subject, but the truth of history requires me to state, that under this strange impression I undressed myself and went to bed, hanging the remnants of my pantaloons on a fence post, believing it to be a chair. Little did I imagine that my bed was Confederate soil, and my shelter the brave o'erhanging firmament, the majestical roof fretted with golden fire. Yet, so it was, and there, upon the all-nourishing bosom of the Confederacy, there on the highway, in the sight of the spires of Madisonville, I lay down under the fence and slept the sleep of intoxicated innocence, dreaming of Jeff. Davis, the Confederate States of America, Constantine, Temperance, Bacchus, and Macpherson.

Now it was that a wonderful vision broke upon my bewildered gaze, which I fear the English language is too feeble to describe. Nevertheless, I will try.

Nox erat. The moon arose cloudless. At a little before seven o'clock two bright spots, about twelve degrees, were visible, one north and the other south, and immediately a cross was seen in the heavens, the moon joining the four arms of the cross. About half-past eight o'clock the northern light went out, but the cross and the spot to the south remained until past ten, when I became too drunk to look at it longer, and retired again to the soil of the Confederacy.

The vision, according to the best of my recollection,
which, I admit, is somewhat obscure, presented the following appearance :

J

D

'EN TOU- 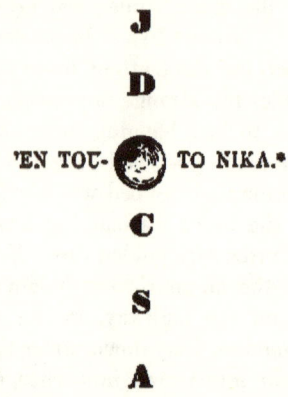 TO NIKA.*

C

S

A

As I have already stated, the northern light went
out at half-past eight o'clock, and by casting his eyes
at the above diagram of the vision, the reader will perceive that the northern light was Jeff. Davis.

Having gone to sleep at half-past ten, I turned un-
easily on the soil and partially awoke, exclaiming:
"Heaven sends miraculous signs whereby it maketh
known its approval of the Confederacy. I will imbrue
my hands in Yankee blood, and do such sanguinary
deeds as will make the name of Macpherson synonymous with human gore. My new shoes shall become
slippery with homicidal claret."

* "With this you will conquer." The words seen by Constantine
on the cross in the sky.

Advent of the Arizonian Gorilla.

Just at this stage of my patriotic address, I was interrupted by a voice like that of Mars, when he roared amid the ranks of the contending Greeks and Trojans, far on the ringing plains of windy Troy. It said :

" Death to the ' American fanatic and the blind and vindictive Unionist !' "

" That remark," I replied, arousing myself, " is a quotation from the *True Delta's* editorial of the 12th inst. Allow me to inquire to whom you refer in that noble and patriotic expression ?"

" To you, vile abolition renegade !—you, ' American fanatic and blind and vindictive Unionist !'—you, impudent hireling of Abraham Lincoln, a bloodier despot than Nero—a man whose shameless and sanguinary deeds, compared with those of Caligula or Heliogabalus, stand black as a Congo African beside a spotless maiden !"

" Allow me to inquire," I responded, " to whom I am indebted for the expression of these noble and patriotic sentiments, at this lonely hour, while the celestial vision whispers peace to my Confederate bosom ?"

" I am the Arizonian," he shouted, while the woods trembled with the roar of his beautiful voice ; " I am the Chief Gorilla, whose will is Confederate law. I am the bloody avenger of my country's wrongs—the gobbler-up of Yankee emissaries and Era correspondents, whose purpose to tear out thy vile heart is as relentless as destiny. I am Don Antonio Maria de Santiago Sibley !" And then he smote his breast and howled.

"Pardon me," I replied, "for interrupting you; but allow me to inquire if you have the latest news through Southern sources?"

He then drew from his pocket the latest *Memphis Appeal,* and read as follows:

"We have to record a great Confederate victory over the Hessians, at Madisonville, but the lateness of the hour and the scarcity of rum will not permit us to give full details. Suffice it to say that Gen. Bragg passed through Madisonville on the 12th inst. with a force of four hundred thousand volunteers, and after marching forty-five miles encountered the Yankees with greatly superior numbers. The fight lasted eighteen hours, and the Yankees were totally routed.

"On the first discharge of our musketry, fifteen thousand Ohio troops fell dead. At the close of the engagement we buried two hundred and eighty-seven thousand of the enemy's slain. Not a man was hurt on our side, notwithstanding we were exposed to a terrible and destructive fire from the enemy's batteries for a day and a half.

"Nine hundred batteries, two hundred thousand prisoners, a million stand of arms, nineteen major-generals, and thirty thousand commissioned officers are among the spoils of our victory. The commissioned officers will be turned over to Gov. Moore for execution, and the privates will be offered double pay and commissions to join the Confederate service.

"Gen. Bragg will reach New Orleans on the 13th inst., at daylight.

"Stonewall Jackson is at Madisonville with eighty-four thousand prisoners.

Later.

"Not one of the enemy survived. Those who were not killed were mortally wounded.

"England has recognized the Southern Confederacy, and a French fleet has blockaded New York and Philadelphia. Lincoln is a prisoner.

Still Later.

"We regret to learn that Gen. Bragg's victory was not so decisive as at first supposed. He has fallen back upon Madisonville, and thinks he will be able to hold his position.

Latest.

"The enemy is in full possession of the field, and has advanced two miles. It is believed that Gen. Bragg's loss is but little more than that of the enemy. Full particulars in our next edition."

As the Gorilla read the above reliable intelligence, I had an opportunity to survey the extraordinary person before me. His brow was dark almost to blackness; his shoulders were as broad as those of Hercules; his breast was covered with a shaggy Confederate blanket, and his breeches were made of leather. His beard and hair nearly swept the ground, while his head was surmounted by a hat with a broad and dilapidated brim. He carried a lasso in his hand, and hurling it with Arizonian agility, he caught me round the neck and drew me to his horse's feet with the strength of Dr. Windship. He then ordered me to prepare to march immediately to the place of execution.

The Vision Explained.

As I took my unmentionables from the fence, I found,
much to my astonishment, that the two arms of the
cross disappeared, and I discovered that the fence stake
on which they had been hanging, formed the upright
part of the great celestial vision, and that the moon,
shining through the large hole in the above-mentioned
garment, had given it the appearance of joining the
four arms of the cross, while the Greek inscription and
the cabalistic letters were easily accounted for by the
vividness of my imagination, and the presence of the
Picayune in one of my pockets.

"Idiot!" shouted the Gorilla, "mount a steed and
make haste, for to-morrow thou shalt die." I obeyed,
and we started off, the squadron all singing a song of
which I remember only the following:

> "I am the bold Gorilla;
>   I wears a ragged shirt;
> My face is like Attila,
>   All covered o'er with dirt.
>
> ' Upon the Mississippi,
>   I walk along so sly,
> A-watching for to whip a
>   Gunboat a-sailing by.
>
> "We've stolen many chickens,
>   We've emptied many a cup;
> We've given the Yankees lickings;
>   We are the Gobblers-up!"

This beautiful and patriotic song was interrupted by
the sight of a telegraph pole, which immediately inspired the Gorilla and his followers with uncontrollable

rage. "Cut the connection!" was the shout, and dashing boldly forward in line, they demolished the telegraph pole, and cut the wire in thirty-five pieces with their sabres; after which we resumed our march, over rough and dangerous roads, impenetrable swamps, and impassable bayous, occasionally stopping to turn a family out of the house, or to rob a hen-roost.

In nineteen hours we arrived at the place of execution—a beautiful and romantic spot, surrounded by mud and overhung with cypress-trees. "Now," said the Arizonian, "prepare for instant death!"

"Is there nothing," I asked, "that will change thy relentless purpose?"

"Nary," he replied. "I am a patriot, and no base considerations move me. I despise the Yankees for their speculations—their mean tricks of traffic; I hate them, because they may be approached with bribes, and will sell out for gold or greenbacks. But, as for me," he continued, haughtily smiting his bosom, "I am swayed only by chivalric devotion to my country. I was educated at West Point, at the expense of the United States, and think I got the best of the Yankees when I turned against them, notwithstanding their shrewdness. So did Beauregard. But to what didst thou allude, Macpherson, when thou didst ask if any thing might not change my purpose?"

"I alluded," was my answer, "to the condition of the exchequer. I know that such patriots must live, and that Confederate hen-roosts are much exhausted, and on condition that you spare my valuable life, I will contribute to your financial resources."

"Hast a gold watch?" asked the unselfish patriot.

"I have.".

"Hast greenbacks?"

"I have."

"Greenbacks," quoth the Gorilla, "are not as good as New Orleans shinplasters and car-tickets. I prefer ragged three-dollar bills cut in two in the middle, for they remind me of charity concerts, the proceeds of which are used to clothe Confederate prisoners."

"Thy wish shall be gratified, most noble of patriots!" I answered; "I will give thee my gold watch, and $50 in cut bills, in exchange for my valuable life."

"I consider I have got the best of the bargain," said the Gorilla, as he smilingly appropriated the money and watch. "Macpherson, thou hast paid more than thy life is worth."

I then returned to Madisonville, thinking of the noble patriotism of those men, actuated only by the love of the new nation, and longing in my heart to kill a Yankee or destroy a telegraph pole.

Yours, perseveringly,

JAMES B. MACPHERSON.

CHAPTER VI.

A Full Account of the Great Macpherson Festival at the House of the Noble Woman, in New Orleans.

Note.—Previous to the departure of the British war-vessel Rinaldo from the port of New Orleans, in the spring of 1863, a party was given to the officers of that ship at the house of a secessionist, in great secrecy. The officers had, on every occasion, exhibited their sympathy for the rebel cause, and the party was composed only of faithful secessionists. The toasts, songs, and all proceedings were of the worst rebel description. A flag of the United States was thrown under the table, where all present trampled upon it, and the rebel colors were displayed and honored.——The tickets of the New Orleans City Railroad Company are used for small change, their value being a picayune—five cents.——At the time this letter was written, the secessionists confidently expected "Stonewall" Jackson to capture the city. Indeed, the race of those who expect to see the rebel power re-established in New Orleans, is not yet extinct ; but as the armies of the "Confederacy" are driven back and defeated by our forces, the rumors of large rebel armies, just ready to dash in upon the city, become more vague and less frequent.

MADISONVILLE, LA.,
March 21st, 1863.

Sir :—I arrived in New Orleans on Saturday, accompanied by my Idiotic Boy, and had scarcely registered my name at the St. Charles, when I was immediately surrounded by a great crowd of admiring friends, who thanked me for my able defense of the Confederacy, and for my brilliant assaults upon the United States. I replied, that the Confederacy alone was worthy of our devotions, and that I received their kind remarks, not as a compliment to me, but to the Confederacy I represented ; and they admitted that such was the fact. I had long believed that I was a

descendant of German ancestors, and in order to settle
the question definitely, I measured heads with a Dutch-
man, and as our heads were exactly of the same size, I
considered my Gothic descent fully established.

But the principal object of my visit to the city was
to accept the invitation of a Noble Woman—a widow,
whose husband has lost his life in the cause of the Confederacy. This lady, charmed both by my patriotism
and my literary abilities, had begged that I would visit
her, in company with my Idiotic Boy, and promised to
give me a grand dinner and festival if I should accept;
and I will now give you a full account of

The Great Macpherson Festival.

I found, on entering the house, that the most elabo-
rate preparations had been made for my reception, and
neither time, car-tickets, nor labor had been spared to
make the occasion worthy of the great purpose.

A mammoth hoop-skirt had been manufactured ex-
pressly for the banquet, so large that it filled the whole
room. This was spread over the table and surmounted
by a Confederate flag a hundred and sixty feet long,
the whole forming a beautiful and spacious canopy.
The Noble Woman and her daughters had a Confederate flag in each breadth of skirt, while a miniature
flag-staff had been fixed into the back of their heads,
from which gracefully streamed the emblem of the new
nation, and saucy rebel rosettes covered their craniums,
beautifully mingling and contrasting the Confederate
colors with the darkness of their shining raven locks.

The concave of the spacious canopy was decorated

with appropriate mottoes and inscriptions, painted in beautiful red ink, which would make a column of the Era; but I shall give only a few of the most striking, to-wit:

> "Oh, welcome, great Macpherson !
> Our hearts no more are light ;
> We breathe a bitter curse on
> Our Yankee foes to-night."

"The Confederacy: It must and shall be preserved."—*Andrew Jackson Davis.*

"Die, Base Yankee Dog !"—*James B. Macpherson.*

"I am Opposed to Negroes in the Abstract."—*Ibid.*

As I entered the house, followed by my Idiotic Boy, the Noble Woman advanced, and bowing in a stately and inviting manner, said : "Welcome, great Confederate !—Literary Light of Madisonville and New Orleans ! —you who have defended us when our rights were in peril, and stood up to the scratch when Lovell sold the city to Farragut !—we wish to pay a tribute to your great abilities, which is only equalled by your devotion to the Confederacy." To which I replied, that I did not regard this as a compliment to me personally, but to the Confederacy I represented. A nigger fiddler, who had been hired for the performance, now struck up *Beauregard's March*, and we all danced a jig around the table.

A retired and secluded residence had been selected, and the door was locked, double-bolted, and chained, while the windows were barricaded with empty barrels and cotton bales, to hide the light and prevent the noise being heard outside. "These precautions are necessary," said the Noble Woman, "because the people of New Orleans live in a condition of abject bondage. We are not permitted to arm ourselves against the United States, nor to keep heavy ordnance in our houses preparatory to a Confederate insurrection, nor can we have Confederate processions unless we attend funerals, nor boldly hurrah for Jeff. Davis."

"Unhappy people!" I exclaimed, my heart wrung with the deepest pity; "you remind me of Prometheus, the son of Iapetus, and the instructor of mortals, who is said to have surpassed all men in sagacity. For having brought fire from heaven to earth in a hollow cane, he was chained to a rock with an eagle to prey upon his liver. Even so, enslaved ones, are you bound to an unhappy destiny, with bands of iron and hooks of steel, and the American eagle is gnawing out your vitals. But let not your hearts be filled with despair, for in thirty thousand years Hercules, the son of Jupiter, hastened to his relief, snapped asunder his bonds, and he, Prometheus still, arose clothed with all the dignity of Southern independence. And as promptly as Hercules hastened to the relief of Prometheus, shall Stonewall Jackson come to snap the Yankee bonds which chain this enslaved people to an unhappy destiny, and you shall arise and shine in the light of the Confederacy! He may be expected Anno Domini 31,863, if nothing happens, meantime, to prevent. Were it not for the scarcity of provisions existing at Madisonville, I would invite the enslaved populace to visit that classical town, and extend to all the freedom of the city in a box. But at present that is impracticable."

A great many guests had been invited, male and female, and all of them first-class Confederates, and neutral citizens and foreign subjects. No small fry were present, I assure you.

I was introduced to each one, and they all complimented me until I blushed; but I told them I did not consider it a compliment to me personally, but to the Confederacy which I represented.

At last the time came for dinner, and we formed a procession in the parlor and marched in under the magnificent canopy. As I entered the room, the nigger struck up, "Hail to the Chief!" when the whole assembly gave three cheers for Macpherson and Jeff. Davis. I replied: "I thank you for these manifestations of your kindness, but I do not consider it a compliment to me personally, but to the Confederacy which I represent." Whereupon we all sat down.

Two niggers then entered the room with a United States flag in a miniature coffin. It was taken out and spread under the table, and we all tramped on it. Then the nigger played the *Mansfield Lovell Quickstep up the Jackson Railroad*, when the Noble Woman said: "Ladies and gentlemen—we have assembled this night to honor the great light of Confederate literature, James B. Macpherson. [Deafening sensation.] I have erected this hoopskirt canopy as an appropriate emblem of the courage, valor, and daring deeds of the Confederates who still reside in New Orleans. For, to the disgrace of the United States be it said, such is the uninterrupted and infamous tyranny under which we groan, that the brave sons of the Confederacy who now inhabit this unhappy city, and even French subjects and British

3

sailors, are compelled to seek protection and safety amid the skirts of our beautiful women ; and here alone it is, in secluded places, with double-bolted doors and barricaded windows, with hushed voices and throbbing hearts, stimulated by champagne and nigger-fiddling, and overshadowed and concealed by a mammoth skirt, that we are permitted to trample upon the flag of the United States, that detestable emblem of despotism, whose stripes are painted with innocent Confederate blood, and whose stars are more malignant than Sirius !"

As the Noble Woman uttered the closing sentence of her eloquent invective, an electric shock of patriotic rage ran around the table, similar to that which one would experience holding on to a galvanic battery or grabbing the electric eel, and rising to our feet we swore eternal and undying devotion to the Confederacy. The Noble Woman then said that as I had not had any thing to eat for several days, I had better proceed uninterruptedly with my dinner, and speak afterward. To which I replied that I did not regard it as a compliment to me personally, but to the Confederacy which I represented. Having eaten, the cloth was removed, and then it was that the fun commenced. The first regular toast was given by the Noble Woman. It was

"MACPHERSON."

The whole assembly arose, and I was drunk standing, when the audience called out: "Speech !" To which I replied : "I thank you, enslaved citizens of New Orleans, lovely women with shining locks, and eyes radiant with beauty, countenances rivalling those which come to us in our dreams of fairy-land—brave and stalwart men, devoted to the Confederacy, but prudently waiting for the coming of Stonewall Jackson before you risk your lives in the glorious cause—French subjects and English mariners, justly abusive towards the United States, and enjoying its protection—I thank you all for this spontaneous and undeserved manifestation of your good-will, but I do not regard it as a compliment to me personally, but to the Confederacy I represent."

The second regular toast was then announced:

"DEATH TO THE YANKEES."

Drunk standing, and music by the nigger.

Third regular toast: "CONFUSION TO FARRAGUT."

At the mention of this name the whole assembly turned pale, except the nigger, who instantly struck up the *Ram Hollins Polka.* Unable to restrain my rage, I emptied two bottles without stopping.

Fourth regular toast: "JEFF. DAVIS AND THE SOUTHERN CONFEDERACY—may they float over the North American continent, so long as a loyal Confederate is hunting for the last ditch."

Air: *Bragg's Murfreesboro' Lament.*

Fifth regular toast: "THE PRESS OF NEW ORLEANS."

Response by my Idiotic Boy, James Buchanan Macpherson, Jr., whose noble and patriotic address was received with shouts of applause; and the moment my Idiotic Boy sat down, he was surrounded by the greatest secessionists of the city, and by foreign subjects, who shook him by the hand, and told him he talked much like their greatest sages, that he ought no longer to be called an idiot.

But a chap who hadn't said much previously, but had sat reading the newspapers, approached me and said: "Mr. Macpherson—for *your* genius and patriotism I have the greatest respect; but as for your boy, he is a humbug. The speech which he palmed off on the audience is not original, but was stolen bodily from the *Picayune's* editorials of the 17th and 19th inst., with a few alterations for the better; and for my part, I consider the young man's idiocy fully established." He then handed me copies of the papers referred to, and, upon examining them, I found that my poor boy had copied his speech, word for word, from them, with some trifling alterations, and I ordered him to leave the house. "The name of Macpherson," I said, "is the synonym of honor, and the undying antagonist of plagiarism, and I do this to show you that the man whom you this night feed, will sacrifice paternal endearment to the principles of integrity."

Volunteer toasts were now called for, and arising with my most fascinating bow, I proposed, "THE LADIES." To which the Noble Woman responded: "The ladies of this City, that is, them that deserves to be called ladies, is true to the Confederacy; for the moment that a female is decently civil to a Yankee, she should, and in my estimation does, forfeit the name of lady. I hope the time will come when, like the royal Saxons, from whom we have descended, we may drink champagne from the skulls of our enemies; and when the freedom of speech and of the press shall be restored, so that those who whisper Union may be hung to a lamp-post."

As the Noble Woman uttered these sublime and patriotic sentiments, I was animated with overpowering admiration, and springing to my feet, I cried: 'O Hebe! step-daughter of cloud-compelling Jove, and spouse of serpent-strangling Hercules, now indeed do I believe that Jupiter dismissed thee from the skies, and sent thee to New Orleans! Such elevated sentiments as the beautiful being before me has expressed, could not have emanated from lips wholly mortal, and verily do I believe that the sweet orator who just took her seat is the Hebe of the South, crowned with immortal youth!"

Champagne now flowed down the table in torrents, and the scene became one of unalloyed enjoyment. Youth, beauty, genius, there mingled together in songs of sweet accord to the Confederacy, until one by one the guests disappeared, leaving me alone beneath the spacious canopy, with an unfinished bottle before me. I tried to think of a subject for my next letter, but all was dim, uncertain, and confused. As clouds driven by the winds chase each other fitfully across the pale moon's face, even so flitted the thoughts and visions of the undersigned; and as the hollow sea at last engulfs the wrecked mariners struggling vainly for life, even so were the thoughts of Macpherson, vainly struggling for shape, form, and consistency, lost in the wide ocean of unconsciousness.

And in conclusion, let me warn young men never to drink any thing intoxicating; for now it was that the name of Macpherson was first brought into disgrace. I fell under the table in a condition of drunken insensibility, from which I was partially aroused the next morning by a scream from the Noble Woman and her daughters.

They, in fact, entered the dining-room the next morning after the great festival, and there discovered me stretched upon the floor, with the detested flag which we had so eagerly trodden under foot wrapped about my person, as I had mistaken it for a Confederate blanket. Incensed at an insult so gross, the Noble Woman and her daughters, without giving me time to arouse and explain, fell upon me with broomsticks and pokers, driving me into the street. I was still too drunk to realize what had happened, and actually walked the whole length of Canal-street wrapped in the folds of that detested flag, exciting the admiration of all Yankees, the indignation of Confederates, the grin of darkies, and the loud yells of a procession of boys who followed me to my lodgings. There my Idiotic Boy tore the hated emblem from the person of his venerated father, and we put back to Madisonville, without stopping once to drink.

Yours in disgrace,
JAMES B. MACPHERSON.

CHAPTER VII.

MACPHERSON SETTING UP AS A CONFEDERATE PHILOSOPHER
EXPLAINS THE DISTINCTION OF RACES TO HIS IDIOTIC BOY.
—ADVENT, HISTORY, AND ADVENTURES OF THE UNHAPPY
CUSS.—MACPHERSON CAPTURED BY DURYEA'S ZOUAVES.—
INTERVIEW WITH THE "SOUTHERN SOURCE," ETC., ETC.

NOTE.—It is well known that "the chivalry" were accustomed, before the war, to claim for themselves superiority of blood, culture,
and refinement.——The reader will need no instruction to recognize
in the "Unhappy Cuss," a representative of that class of Northerners
who used to come to the South, and change their principles with the
climate; and who were prepared to change them as often as their
pecuniary interests required.——Contraband trade across Lake Pontchartrain was carried on to a considerable extent, and at great risk;
the cargoes frequently falling into the hands of the military. But
when the rascals succeeded in eluding the military and getting their
cargoes into the market, they realized rich returns.——About the
time this letter was written, Pontchatoula, a village in Eastern
Louisiana, was captured by an expedition under Colonel Clark, consisting of the Sixth Michigan regiment and the Second Duryea's
Zouaves (165th New York).——"News through Southern Sources,"
was the title under which the secession press of New Orleans was accustomed to publish the mild sensation reports of rebel victories
that were sent from Jackson and Mobile, to comfort the faithful secessionists of the Crescent City. These reports were frequently without
the slightest foundation in truth, and the "Southern Source" became
the synonym of unblushing mendacity.

MADISONVILLE, LA.,
March 28th, 1863.

SIR :—It was a cloudless and lovely afternoon, and a
refreshing breeze brought to my nostrils all the com-
mingled odors of Madisonville, as I sat in the open door
of my Hospitable Abode, half asleep. My mind wandered
back to Plato, the greatest philosopher of the Greeks, and

I therefore determined to set up as a Confederate Philosopher. It was not long before an opportunity of entering upon this new and honorable career presented itself; for my Idiotic Boy approached and asked me what a Yankee is. I replied: "An abolitionist."

"What is an abolitionist?" inquired the imbecile youth.

"A Hessian," I answered.

"What is a Hessian?" persisted the youth.

"Sweet Idiot!" I said, "the human family is divided into two great classes—Southerners and Yankees. The Southerners are a superior race, and inevitable gentlemen. On the other hand, all who are not born inside the Confederate lines are Yankees, Abolitionists, and Hessians, which, in the Confederate lexicon, are synonymous terms. The Yankees are an inferior race by birth, and are forever unfit to associate on terms of social equality with Southerners. My advice to all future generations is, Be born in the Confederacy. Otherwise, they will lack that chivalric and indescribable grace which belongs to every white man born in the Confederacy—that charm which clings to your revered father, and which, thank heaven, I can visibly trace in thee, my poor, Idiotic Boy."

Advent of the Unhappy Cuss.

The Idiot wept for joy, and clasping him to my bosom in a glow of paternal pride and fondness, we mingled our Confederate tears together, when the touching and beautiful scene was interrupted by the approaching footsteps of a stranger, whose grief-stricken countenance unmistakably indicated that he was the Unhappy Cuss.

"Who art thou? whence comest, and whither goest?"
I inquired.

"I am," he answered "a victim of the greatest misfortune that can fall to the lot of articulate-speaking men!"

"Alas! wretched one," I answered, "make known the cause of this calamity, and I pledge my assistance."

"Thanks, generous and sublime Macpherson!" quoth the stranger, "great and admired Confederate philosopher, for thy proffered help; but, alas! my malady is beyond mortal aid!"

"Unhappy Cuss!" I exclaimed, in a tone of meek pity; "Despair is the twin-brother of Death, and the system of philosophy I am about to bring to light, embraces this great principle, that when a man won't stand by himself, no one is longer obligated to stand by him."

"Wisest of all Confederates!" responded the Unhappy Cuss, "greatest of living teachers! thy maxims of philosophy may place thy name on record as the Confederate Plato, but they cannot heal a bleeding spirit, nor bind up a wounded heart. My malady is of the blood; I inherited it at birth; I inhaled it with the air I breathed, and no medicine in the world can do me good."

"Explain," I said, "this leprous distilment which hath blighted thy young hopes. Speak, Unhappy Cuss!"

"I will unfold to thee the great secret of my life," quoth he; "but let me whisper it, for I have not the courage to pollute the air with these fearful words. He then rolled over three times in the dirt, and placing

his lips close to my ear, while a look of ghastly despair
flitted across his protruding under-jaw, whispered these
fearful words :

"*I have Yankee blood in my veins !*"

As the Unhappy Cuss said the above words, he was
seized with spasms, and fell rolling in the dust at my
feet. The Idiotic Boy, who had been a silent but tearful spectator of the scene, immediately threw a barrel
of rain water upon his prostrate form, and I rubbed his
head with an inkstand until consciousness once more
returned.

History of the Unhappy Cuss.

He then proceeded to unfold his woful tale. " I
am," he said, " a native of Connecticut. My ancestors
came from England in the Mayflower. They were, in
fact, adherents of those detestable Puritans and Roundheads, who had the insolence to overthrow a King, and
cut his head off to boot. I was taught to believe in
those bloody wretches for saints, and I also thought
that the American Union was the greatest monument
of wisdom and liberty ever erected by the hands of
mortal men. Every 4th of July I was drunk for a
week in honor of George Washington and the United
States, and ' Yankee Doodle' was my favorite air.

" Fortune at last decreed that I should leave my
native land and come to New Orleans. As I stood on
the deck of the vessel, and saw the hills of New England sink in the distant horizon, my eyes were filled
with tears, and I vowed that never, while life should
last, would I prove recreant in thought or deed, to
those great principles of national unity which were so

impressed upon my affections. But the moment the warm breezes of the South touched me, I began to realize a change. It seemed to me that the Roundheads ought to have been whipped by the Cavaliers, and that virtue triumphed with the restoration of Stuart's cavalry.

"The instant I set foot on the levee at New Orleans, the scales fell from my eyes, and I was seized with shame for my Yankee blood. I swore that I hated Yankees, and this patriotic sentiment grew day by day until it goaded me on to deeds of bloodshed and theft. I carefully studied the habits of Southern society, and carried a revolver in each breeches pocket, and a bowie-knife and corn-cutter in my belt. I knocked down a nigger and cursed the Yankees at every public gathering; and when secession got under way, I hung three Union men to a lamp-post with my own hands, stole five thousand dollars in cash, and out-confederated the Confederates in my devotion to Southern independence."

As the Unhappy Cuss closed his narrative, a glow of Confederate pride overspread his features, and my classical mind arose to the full height of the sublime occasion. "Benignant stranger!" I exclaimed, "such is the glory of the Confederacy that its light strikes dumb every Yankee who sets foot upon its sacred soil, and he cannot wag his tongue except in praise of the Confederacy. I hail thee, Unhappy Cuss, as a Confederate Yankee. But you will excuse me if I decline to introduce you to Mrs. Macpherson; for while I admit the great worth of a man who is ready to fight and steal for the Confederacy, I cannot welcome him on terms of social equality, if he has Yankee blood in his veins."

Mrs. Macpherson now entered the house and turned
up her nose at the Yankee Cuss, and remarked that the
person could sit down at the second table.

The next day was Jeff. Davis's fast and humiliation,
and the Cuss and I went to church. The parson
preached from the words: "*Hold fast.*" It was very
convenient, for we had nothing in the house to eat, and
I could starve the guest without a violation of the laws
of hospitality. We both got drunk, however, as a Confederate humiliation, and the Cuss opened to me a
great plan of speculation.

"I have," he said, "a scheme of wealth, which will
make us both richer than Judah P. Benjamin. Philosophy is good in its way, but let me tell you, Macpherson, that philosophy don't pay. Hast thou Confederate treasury notes?"

"I have only $95,000 by me at present," I replied.

"That is just the amount I want," answered the
Cuss. "I have run the blockade with a satchel of
quinine and salt, which cost me $150 in New Orleans,
and which I have already disposed of for $150,000. I
want $95,000 more, which will enable me to buy a
schooner and load her with cotton, and with this I will
run the blockade and sell it in New Orleans, and will
divide the profits, which will be perfectly enormous."

"Give me thine honest hand!" I cried aloud.

"Give me thy treasury notes!" responded the Unhappy Cuss.

I gave him all the money I had in the world, and we
immediately started for Pontchatoula. We hid in a
swamp, and waded in the water above our knees for
twenty-four hours, in order to escape observation, until

we found a man who was ready to deal with us, and it was not long before a schooner was filled with cotton ready for shipment. I noticed that the Cuss made the purchase entirely in his own name, and did not recognize me at all, except to make me run of errands. When I required an explanation of this, he replied in the following noble and patriotic words:

"You, Macpherson," he said, "are too great a man to mix yourself up with the affairs of material wealth. That occupation belongs wholly to the Yankee mind. You, who are a great philosopher, and in whose veins courses only Confederate blood, should not bend the gigantic intellectual energies of your mammoth brain to any such grovelling object. No, no!—leave that to *me*, and I'll fix the thing for you."

As he was paying this just tribute to my intellectual worth, the earth suddenly trembled beneath our feet, as if suffering in the throes of mortal agony; while a howl of terror and frenzied panic rolled through the swamp in which we were situated. A whizzing noise penetrated the branches of the trees, and pale with abject fear, we saw the Gorillas dashing wildly through the woods in confusion, crying out in tones like those of Stentor, the Grecian warrior whose voice was louder than the combined voice of fifty men:

"The Yanks! the Yanks are upon us!"

On they flew, like the winds, while the Unhappy Cuss and myself, were transfixed to the earth, with amazement and fright. Soon the woods around us flashed with the fire of musketry, and the highway swarmed with the red-breeches, which, in my terror, I believed to be devils, like those in the opera, who carry

off Don Giovanni, as he is taking a drink of champagne.
The next thing in the strange chapter of my adventures, I was surrounded by a squad of the red-breeches,
with fierce looks and flashing bayonets, who demanded
an immediate and unconditional surrender to Duryea's
Zouaves. I replied that the proud chivalric blood of
Macpherson, was at any time prepared to be shed for
the Confederacy, but that while I had a leg to stand on,
or an arm to smite with, I would never surrender to a
Yankee.

Macpherson a Captive.

"Fiddlesticks!" replied the Zouave, rapping me on
the head with the butt of his musket. My hands were
then tied behind me and I was carried to the commanding officer, a prisoner of war. But let it be known to
all men forever, that I did not make any formal surrender.

I then looked around me to learn the destiny of the
Unhappy Cuss, and expected to see him hanging to a
limb. I knew that the Yankees prosecute this war on
a plan of such bloody and barbarous ferocity, that
neither of us had the slightest chance of life. Imagine
my amazement, therefore, when I saw the Unhappy
Cuss seated on a log, side by side with a Yankee officer,
taking a drink, and conversing in the most friendly
manner.

"I am glad to see you here," I heard him say to the
vile Yankee. "I have a load of cotton here ready to
be shipped to New Orleans, and I have been waiting
my opportunity for several weeks to slip off with it, and
now I shall be able to do so. I hail you as a deliverer

from the cruel oppressions of the traitors; there is not
an impulse in my heart which is not true to the flag of
the Union. Let's take a drink!"

"Liar! Base dog!" I exclaimed, "the cotton is mine,
and you are a Confederate according to your own con-
fessions."

"Who is that?" asked the Yankee officer, pointing
to me.

"A crazy man whom I hired by the day to watch
my cotton," replied the Cuss, "but I discharged him
for evident insanity."

Reader! are you human? Has your compassion
been eviscerated? Think of such an insult to me, the
great light of Confederate literature, and the Plato of
Madisonville, and weep with pity for the depravity of
man. My hands were untied, and I was told to go
home, for the Yankee commander said he pitied an in-
sane man; to which the Unhappy Cuss responded that
for this reason he pitied the whole Confederacy.

"Good by, Macpherson," he said. "I am grateful
for your hospitality, and I admit the inferiority of the
Yankee race."

"Liar!—swindler!—thief!—traitor!—villain!" I replied, and started for home.

Interview with the Southern Source.

As I was going along, I saw a chap dodge from behind a tree in the swamp, and wave his hand to me. I
approached, when in a mysterious tone he whispered:

"I am a Southern Source!"

"What's new, my honest friend?" I asked him.

"Much," he said, at the same time waving a news-paper before my eyes. I reached out to look at it, when he suddenly slipped off and put the paper in his pocket. "Seven hundred and ninety dollars," said he. "The brokers in New Orleans will give me $800, but I will take $790 here."

"I must first know whether the news is worth the money," I answered.

"Did ever a Southern Source deceive the public?" he inquired. "Is not my name and reputation for veracity a shield against such base imputations? But I will give you one little item to show that the paper is worth it. It contains an account of Jeff. Davis in New York."

"Jeff. Davis in New York!" I exclaimed, raising my hands in gratitude; "then is Pontchatoula aveng-ed!" I borrowed the money, and the Southern Source disappeared, legging it through the woods when last seen.

I proceeded to examine the paper, when I discovered that it was of the 29th October, 1858, and contained an account of Jeff. Davis's speech at a democratic meeting in Palace Garden, New York. Let me tell you that the man who sold that paper upon false pre-tenses, is a disgrace to Southern Sources; for the char-acter of these Sources is above reproach or the sus-picion of falsehood; and whatever you read in a Con-federate newspaper you can safely accept as the unadul-terated gospel of truth.

I must draw my letter to a close. I have once more reached my hospitable abode at Madisonville, and, as I write these closing sentences, I look back upon the ex-

perience of the past week with a philosophic eye.
I have been shamefully swindled by the Unhappy Cuss
and the Southern Source, but my faith in the Confederacy is not dimmed. The light of victory shall flash
upon our banners, and I pledge my word that if the
base Yankee foe ever takes possession of Madisonville,
he will first walk over the prostrate and mangled body
of

Yours, philosophically,

JAMES B. MACPHERSON.

CHAPTER VIII.

THE GREAT CHARITY FAIR.

NOTE.—Mr. N. O. J. Tisdale, formerly President of the New Orleans City Gas Company, and a well-known registered enemy of the United States, who finally left the city and went into the "Confederacy," held a fair at his residence, professedly for the benefit of the Protestant Orphan Asylum, but really, it was generally believed, for the purpose of raising funds with which to clothe the rebel prisoners then in New Orleans. In the name of charity, tickets were sold to all who would purchase, and many Union men and women purchased, not suspecting the true character of the entertainment. The fair was a full-blooded secession demonstration ; the rebel colors were displayed, rebel airs were played on the piano, and certain rebel poems, printed secretly, were sold at twenty-five cents apiece. These poems were entitled respectively, "The Battle of the Handkerchiefs," and "The Battle of the Fair." The authorship is attributed here to Macpherson's Idiotic Boy ; but they were really written by a young lady of New Orleans, who has composed several ingenious secession poems, and who sometimes signs herself Emily M. Washington. Mr. Tisdale was arrested, and his trial, which continued several days, attracted great attention in New Orleans, and was the subject of comment in the Northern papers. While witnesses were brought by the prosecution who swore positively that "The Bonnie Blue Flag" was performed, and other secession demonstrations made, Mr. Tisdale brought witnesses in large numbers, who swore that they neither heard that air, nor witnessed any thing indicating sympathy for the rebel cause. The court, in its decision, acquitted Mr. Tisdale, on the ground that these negative witnesses for the defense were present all the evening, and that it was a moral impossibility that they should not have heard the air had it actually been performed.——The arrest and punishment of the Idiotic Boy for hurrahing for Jeff. Davis, was intended to exhibit the folly of the light punishment of such offenses, which at one time consisted of a small fine. It was currently reported and believed that every fine imposed for such offenses was promptly paid by the secessionists, and a little purse given to the "martyr" as a bounty on impudent treason. It is said that this bounty was sometimes as high as fifty dollars ; so that one who should hurrah for Jeff. Davis could do so without expense to himself, and make a handsome little sum out of it besides.——The author cannot close this note without expressing his admiration for the bold and able manner in which the prosecution in the Tisdale case was conducted by the City Attorney, Mr. L. Madison Day.

MADISONVILLE, LA.,
April 4th, 1863.

Sir: It was midnight, and the pale beams of the heaven-traversing moon shone down upon the pellucid bosom of Lake Pontchartrain, and streamed through the crevices of my Dilapidated, Hospitable Abode, and silence and slumbers prevailed among living men. But I, moved with pity for the wrongs of the Confederacy, and, like much-planning Ulysses, revolving many thoughts in my mind, was no more able to sleep than was Calypso, inconsolable at the departure of her Grecian hero. Therefore, I arose from my lofty couch, and in gloomy meditation, walked to the banks of the Tchefuncta, whose beautiful, muddy water, seemed to be a reflex of my own sombre and philosophic thoughts. Seating myself upon the all-nourishing earth, I thus poured out my soul to the noble river:

"O Tchefuncta! thou, whose beautiful mud is as clear as the hopes of the Confederacy, listen to the moans of thy philosophic son! Tell me, ye lonely depths of dirt! whether in a time of national calamity, with the stars and stripes floating over the blood-stained heights of Pontchatoula, a philosophic mind may devote itself to the pursuit of occult truth, or whether it be not the duty of every Confederate, even though like me, he be gifted with a mammoth brain, to bare his arm in the cause of his country? I pause for a reply."

Having delivered this eloquent apostrophe to the

noble river, I fell partially asleep, when I heard a mysterious voice, crying from the depths:

"Bare the arm! bare the arm!"

"I will!" I responded; "for in that voice I recognize a Confederate sign and miracle, surpassing in wonder the dreams of the *Picayune;* and I shall forthwith proceed with my long-cherished design of forming a Congo Body Guard."

I then went to sleep, when I was suddenly aroused by a kick in the back, which sent me headforemost into the muddy depths of the sluggish Tchefuncta.

"Spirit!" I exclaimed, "who but recently spake to me from these waters, unless, indeed, my eyes were bent on vacancy, and I with incorporeal air did hold discourse, receive thy son, and assist him to reach dry land!" I then waded back, comparing myself to Venus, who rose from the sea, while the moist-blowing west wind wafted her in soft foam along the waves, and the gold-filleted Seasons received her on the shores of Cyprus, clothed her in immortal garments, placed a golden wreath upon her head, and led her to the assembly of the gods. And as I wallowed in the mud of the noble river, I exclaimed: "I am the Venus of Madisonville, arising from the Tchefuncta, and waiting for immortal honors!"

I then stepped upon the bank, when a wild mule kicked at me and brayed, and I found that I had mistaken the mule's familiar voice for a Confederate miracle, and that the heels of the said animal had given me midnight baptism. Nevertheless, I accepted the advent of the mule as a celestial sign, and immediately mounting the same, I started for New Orleans.

The Solitary Horseman.

I had proceeded seventy-five rods on my journey, when my attention was attracted by the clatter of a horse's hoofs, and soon the Solitary Horseman, whose appearance and history have been fully described by the late Mr. James, burst upon my vision. Immediately I apostrophized him as the Confederacy, for the seal of the New Nation is to be a Cavalier, and I found the Solitary Horseman to be the *beau ideal* of a Confederate gentleman.

No sooner had I spoken, than he dismounted his foaming steed, and embracing my knees, exclaimed:

"At last I behold thee, Confederate Plato, Venus of Madisonville, and chiefest light of Confederate letters! I am the delegate of three thousand citizens of New Orleans, who have charged me to express to you the profound respect which they entertain for your august person, and invite you to attend a Grand Charity Fair to-morrow evening, at the residence of a gentleman whose heart is as true to the Confederacy as is Jacob Barker's to his safe. Charity," continued the Cavalier, "like the dews of heaven, falls upon the lowly and the poor; and when I think of the hard lot of the unhappy orphan, cast upon the heartless world without a guiding and protecting hand, my heart is torn with a thousand pangs of agony, and the hot blood goes rushing wildly through my swollen veins. O Macpherson! let us weep for the unhappy lot of the poor and debased orphan!"

The Solitary Horseman burst out in a fit of inconsolable tears as he uttered this sublimely charitable sen-

timent, and I was about to press his gentle hand in
mine, when the Wild Mule gave an awful kick which
frustrated my affectionate design. The brave Cavalier
then mounted and we dashed furiously along the highway.

" Is this Fair political ?" I asked.

" It is charitable, charitable, Macpherson," he replied
—" a Fair in behalf of the Protestant Uniform Asylum, an institution for the manufacture of graybacks,
where the weary Confederate may find rest, and the
naked Confederate may become clothed."

" Who hath contributed thereunto ?" I inquired.

Much to my astonishment, the tender-hearted Cavalier burst out in a fit of uncontrollable laughter, which
arose far above the clatter of his horse's hoofs. "That's
the joke !" he shouted, as his beautiful laugh rolled
through the lonely swamp; "that's the joke !—the
Yankees have contributed ! Tickets were sold for ten
cents apiece, and in the blessed name of Charity, sweet
mother of the helpless, we sold many tickets to Union
men and women, and Yankee officers !"

Reining in my Wild Mule, I cried aloud : "Then
indeed do I wash my hands of this matter ; for I will
take no part in a Fair, even for Charity, if base Yankee
gold is mingled with the spotless currency of the Confederacy !"

The Cavalier whistled, as he drew from his pocket a
Richmond Examiner, and read the price of gold, $5.25,
and an advance of two hundred per cent. in a week.
" Be not too hasty, Confederate Plato," he observed.
" You are aware that the end justifies the means ; and
in the present instance the great end to be achieved is

to clothe the Confederacy. To rob a Yankee or to deceive a Yankee is the highest virtue of the Confederacy. And since the grinding tyranny of the United States will not permit us to operate openly, we invoke the broad mantle of Charity, which we will cut up and make into Confederate uniforms!"

"Give me thine honest hand, sweet messenger of benevolence!" I exclaimed. "Charity, indeed, shall cover a multitude of sins; and the mantle of Charity is gray in the Confederacy."

It was night before we reached the city, and as the mud of the Tchefuncta still adhered conspicuously to my person, I determined to go to the St. Charles and take a bath before attending the Fair. But as we were riding towards that massive structure, the Solitary Horseman suddenly reined in his steed, and pointing to a palatial abode, said: "This is the place—listen!"

A confused din of lovely voices, strains of angelic music, and trippings of the light fantastic toe came to my ears, grateful as the odor of Louisiana Rum to a thirsty Confederate; for I knew that every lovely voice was a Confederate voice, every strain a Confederate strain, and every light fantastic toe a Confederate toe.

Macpherson's Extraordinary Advent at the Fair.

I was about to hasten to the baths, when my Wild Mule kicked with extraordinary violence, lifting me clean from his back, tossing me over the fence and through the open door of the palatial abode, and landing me in the hall on my face, with a force which caused the blood to ooze freely from my nostrils, and

mingle its crimson hues with the mud of the Teche-
functa, which still adhered conspicuously to my person.

The hall was crowded with beautiful Confederate
girls; and as I arose from my recumbent posture,
with my classcial mind slightly confused by the violence of the concussion, I imagined myself in a Vestal
temple. I therefore cried aloud : " O lovely Confederate Vestals, who attend the sacred flame, fear not me,
for I am the Venus of Madisonville; and my only regret is that, placing her hand upon the head of Jupiter,
your goddess swore perpetual celibacy." The Vestals
then joined hands and danced around me, to the en-
livening strains of the *Pontchatoula Quickstep*, and the
Great Host approaching, bade me welcome to the
abode of Charity.

. " Allow me to inquire," I said, "whether you have
obtained permission to hold this Fair?"

"I did not deem it necessary," he replied, "for I
consulted a gentleman who has held a similar concern
at his house, and he assured me that permission was
not necessary. I trust the time will soon come when
we can worship the Confederacy according to the dictates of our own consciences, with none to molest or
make us afraid, and when the ladies can spit in the
face of Yankees in the streets with impunity."

" Amen!" I responded to this noble and patriotic
prayer.

The Great Host lovingly took my arm, and, conduct-
ing me to an obscure corner, pointed in a mysterious
manner to a pile of publications. "To you," he said,
" the great light of Confederate letters, I need not expatiate upon the beauties and blessings of literature; I

need not tell you of the power of the press, which enables us to poison the public mind, and inundate the land with Confederate principles." He then handed me two beautiful Confederate tracts, one them entitled "*The Battle of the Handkerchiefs,*" and the other "*The Battle of the Fair,*" and informed me that the price was two bits each, which sum I gladly paid as he informed me the proceeds of those two beautiful and patriotic publications would go towards clothing the Confederacy.

"Perhaps," he remarked, "you would like to see the author of those great works of genius and patriotism."

"I should rejoice to know him," I replied; "for herein I find the evidences of that peculiar genius and grace which belongs, in a greater or less degree, to every thing Confederate."

"You shall be gratified," he answered; and he immediately led me face to face with my Idiotic Boy!

"There he is!" said the Great Host; "look upon the author of those beautiful productions of the human intellect."

My double surprise may be imagined. I supposed the imbecile youth was quietly sleeping in his mother's arms; but to find him there, surrounded by a galaxy of youth and beauty, and to learn that he was a full-fledged Confederate author, overpowered me with amazement and gratitude. "Happy father of such a son!" I exclaimed, clasping him to my muddy bosom, "who in early life devotes the energies of his idiotic brain to the true path of rectitude, and contributes the efforts of his intellect to the great and heaven-ordained

4

behests of Charity, by furnishing mental pabulum to the followers of the naked Confederacy !"

Just then the Idiot dodged behind me, and pointing to a lady across the room, said : "Shield me, for the love of heaven !"

What is the row, sweet Idiot?" I inquired.

"It is my misfortune to know that lady," he replied. "I have eaten at the same table, drank wine from the same bottle, played whist and euchre with the same cards. But she is a Union woman, and it will be a disgrace to recognize her here."

"Well said, dear Idiot," I responded. "But show yourself worthy of your revered father and of the Confederacy you represent."

"I will !" he exclaimed, tearing his hair with vehement determination, and then walking coldly by the Yankee woman, without recognizing her. Afterwards he watched his opportunity and winked at her, in order, if possible, to save her good opinion without compromising himself.

"Sir !" I said with a frown of Confederate displeasure upon my features, and addressing myself to the Great Host: "You are a registered enemy of the United States, and I was not prepared for the affront put upon me by the presence of a Yankee woman."

"Gas !" responded the Great Host, his eyes gleaming like two burners, "you are over zealous. It is possible that the vile tyranny under which we groan, will summon me to answer for this night's business, and the presence of a few Yankees is a shield against suspicion."

I now proceeded to examine the spacious apartments:

and at every step I found something to gladden my
Confederate heart. I learned that beautiful maidens
of tender years had worked with the mothers of the
city, day after day, and night after night, in manufac-
turing miniature Confederate flags, which they brought
here and sold at high prices, the proceeds all going
into the Confederate treasury. I saw, also, Confederate doll-babies, Confederate roosters and hens, Confederate pigs made of sugar, Confederate dogs, and Confederate alligators, all manufactured by fair hands in
obedience to the dictates of charity. But the principal feature of the evening was a Confederate donkey,
gayly caparisoned, on which sat my Idiotic Boy, waving the proud banner of the New Nation, and winking
at the girls.

The Great Confederate Seal.

"That Donkey and that boy," remarked a bystander,
"are the proper and fitting emblems of the Confederacy. I see that our Congress is discussing the pro-
priety of adopting a Cavalier as the seal of the New
Nation; and I for one recommend Macpherson's Idiotic
Boy mounted on a Donkey as the most expressive and
appropriate Boy and Beast that can be found to represent the Confederacy."

It was suggested that I myself, mounted on my
Wild Mule, would do better; but the opinion of the
audience was in favor of the Idiot, and so I yielded my
claims gracefully, soothing my disappointed ambition
with the gushing stream of paternal pride.

During all this time the piano was sending forth its
angelic strains, the keys thereof being thumbed by

snowy delicate fingers, whose gentle touch upon the
temples might soothe a tiger's rage, or thaw the cold
heart of a conqueror. *The Bonnie Blue Flag* was
played, as the most popular air; but whenever that air
was struck, I observed that twelve persons immediately
left the room, and put cotton in their ears. I demanded of the Great Host the cause of this extraordinary
proceeding, which appeared to me to be an insult to
the Confederacy.

The Great Host applied his forefinger to the side of
his nose, giving the end a twist and winking as he replied:

" Witnesses !"

" What witnesses !" I inquired.

" You see, Macpherson," he replied, " that my case
may come up in court, and it is possible that some who
are here may have the baseness to testify that *The
Bonnie Blue Flag* was performed on that piano.
In such a case it will become necessary for me to prove
that it was NOT played. So I have arranged to have
twelve witnesses be present through the whole performance and *not* hear it. If the tune was actually played
it is morally certain that these twelve persons must
have heard it ; and these witnesses live in a Christian
community, and are, as you will perceive, persons of
the highest respectability. Cotton will do it, Macpherson—cotton will do it !"

" Cotton is king," I answered ; " and your case is
sure to succeed. When I was justice of the peace in
Madisonville, a case came up precisely like yours.
Citizen Jenkins accused my nephew, Peter Macpherson,
of stealing a pig, and brought three creditable witnesses,

who swore positively that they saw Peter steal him.
But Pete brought four men of the highest respectability,
over from New Orleans, who swore quite as positively
that they did *not* see him steal the swinish animal; and
on this testimony I was bound to acquit him. Negative
testimony is sure to win in courts that take a proper
view of events, particularly if the magistrate is an
uncle of the accused, as in the case referred to."

The night wore away, and our delightful Confederate
communion strengthened our weary souls. At a late
hour I was called on for a speech, and wishing to appear in my true character, as a Confederate philosopher,
I proceeded to deliver an original phrenological discourse, on one of the most important bumps which the
human head contains.

Macpherson on Memory.

"Ladies and gentlemen," I said; "proud children of
our great Confederate parent, and you of the rising
generation; as mile-boards are set up on the highway
to indicate the direction in which the roads run, so
hath nature built bumps on the human cranium, to indicate the bent of character, and the destiny of man.

"The most important of these bumps indicates the
organ of Memory; and in looking around on this audience I see by a glance at that bump that you are all
Confederates. The Confederate bump of Memory is
peculiar in this, that it has the gift of remembering
every thing to its own credit and interest, with the
most wonderful distinctness. Indeed, it remembers
more than the facts will justify. At the same time it
is wholly incapable of remembering any thing contrary

to the plans, wishes, principles, and interests of the
Confederacy. For instance, it remembers that George
Washington was a Virginian, and a slaveholder; but
it forgets stubbornly and hopelessly that he was a
strong Union man, and freed his slaves on his death-
bed. It remembers that gold arose in New York to
173, but it forgets that it tumbled down faster than it
rose. It remembers that the Mississippi was sunk at
Port Hudson, but it forgets that the Hartford and Al-
batross went by. It remembers that Beauregard won
the battle of Manassas, but it forgets that the Yankees
whipped the devil out of us at Fort Donelson. Such,
ladies, gentlemen, and rising generation, are the char-
acteristics of the Confederate bump of Memory—char-
acteristics of which I am proud, and which I see per-
vade every head in this great charity fair. Were you
called on to swear to-morrow before a Yankee court,
whether a Confederate flag was displayed here to-night,
could you remember seeing it? No! Were you asked
whether the *Bonnie Blue Flag* was played on that
piano, could you remember that you heard it? No!
Were you asked whether any disloyal sentiment has
been expressed here to-night, could you remember hearing it? No!—for you are all loyal to the great principles of the new nation, and may God bless you, and
the Confederate bump of Memory forever!"

pherso.

"Cott   *Arrest of the Idiotic Boy.*

sure to suc

Madisonville, was received with loud applause, and
Citizen Jenkins o separate, when a clamor arose in the
of stealing a pig, federate rising!—to arms!—to arms!"

I shouted; ' the day of deliverance has come!—Stonewall Jackson has arrived with nineteen hundred thousand patriots!" With this exclamation I rushed into the street, the excited assemblage following at my heels, when I found that my Idiotic Boy had been arrested for hurrahing for Jeff. Davis publicly, and basely imprisoned in a Yankee jail. "Martyr of freedom!" I cried; "I am proud that the spirit of the Macphersons has not been crushed, and I resign thee to a glorious death and a crown of martyrdom!"

I found, however, that the penalty for the offense was $2.50, and soon a purse of $200 was made up, the fine paid, and the boy released, with the balance jingling in his pocket. As he left the court-room he set up another tremendous roar for Jeff. Davis, when he was immediately arrested again, and fined $2.50 more. "I appeal to the Confederates," I said, "to assist my son to get his release from the vile Yankee tyrants." Immediately another contribution of $200 was made up, the fine paid, and the boy released, with a clear balance of $395 in his pocket; and with this we immediately returned to Madisonville.

I must now conclude my eighth epistle to THE ERA. What is writ is writ. Would it were worthier. The winding up reminds me that I am mortal; and as that is a subject I do not like to reflect upon, I turn my philosophic eye to the unfading glory of the Confederacy, and there I behold unending power and immortal honor. The stars shall fade, but the Confederacy shall endure forever.

Yours, weekly,
JAMES B. MACPHERSON.

P. S.—Since writing the above, I have received the following letter from my son Louis T. Wigfall:

PORT HUDSON, April 2.

"DAD:—Give My love to the Great Hoast, and to the bewtiful ladies which attended the Charity Fare. I have received the uniform they sent Me, and it's the only rag of close I've had sense I sold the nine sutes which was given Me by the ladies as I left New Orleans on the Empire Parish.

"While a heart beats in My Bosom, it will vibrate with the Gratitude of

Your patriotic Sun,
LOUIS T. WIGFALL MACPHERSON.

CHAPTER IX.

THE CONFEDERATE ARITHMETIC.

MADISONVILLE, LA.,
April 11th, 1863.

SIR:—On Tuesday last I sat on the bottom of an inverted brass kettle in my door-yard, training up my Idiotic Boy in the way he should go, and rejoicing to find his demented brain so capable of absorbing the ideas which underlie the Confederacy. "I am," I said to him, "the Confederate Archimedes. Never, since this great planetary system was called into existence, has there been a nation whose glory and power could compare with the Confederacy which I represent. Wherever the glorious flag of the new nation floats, freedom of speech and of the press prevails to an alarming extent.

"The resources of the Confederacy are inexhaustible. Ever since the formation of the Union, the South has supported the North; and therefore it was, that as soon as the South withdrew from the concern, the North was reduced to poverty and famine. Grass now grows in Broadway, and in the Central Park of New York. A reliable gentleman who has just returned from that place, assures me that he pastured his horse in front of the Astor House, during his sojourn in that deserted and ruined city.

"But the Confederacy can never become impoverished; and I will now explain to you the principles of
⁂*

the Confederate Arithmetic—principles of the greatest
simplicity, yet productive of astounding results.

"The Confederate Arithmetic has two rules, Multiplication and Subtraction. Multiplication is only employed in the affairs of the Confederacy, and Subtraction in the affairs of the Federals.

The Confederate Multiplication-table.

"The Confederate multiplication-table, my Sweet
Idiot," I continued, "employs two numbers—0 and 50.
0 multiplied by 50 equals 50. 0 represents the basis of
Confederate currency, and by multiplying it by 50 you
get $50 in cash. Multiply this by 50 again, and you
have $2,500; and this once more multiplied by 50,
gives you $125,000; and this again multiplied, gives
you $6,250,000; and so on, until the Confederate Treas-
ury groans beneath its enormous and insupportable
burden of cash.

"The rule here laid down also applies to military
operations. A Colonel sends out a Captain on a scouting expedition, and 0 represents the number of Yankee
prisoners actually captured. This the Captain multiplies by 50, and reports to the Colonel that he has
bagged 50 Yankees. The Colonel then multiplies by
50 in his report to the Brigadier General; the Brigadier
General multiplies by 50 in his report to the Division
General; the Division General multiplies by 50 in his
report to the Commander of the Department; the
Commander of the Department multiplies by 50 in his
report to the Secretary of War; the Secretary of War
multiplies by 50, and sends it to the Jackson *Appeal;*
the editor of that sheet multiplies by 50 and prints it,

and the Southern Source then multiplies by 50 and starts for New Orleans, and by the time the report gets to the St. Charles Hotel, we have captured thirty-five trillion sixty-two billion and five hundred million (35,062,500,000,000) Yankee prisoners, as any one will see who will work out the sum according to the principles of the Confederate Arithmetic.

"Every thing in the Confederacy is multiplied by 50. But when we speak of the affairs of the United States, we apply the second great rule of the Confederate Arithmetic, which is as follows:

Confederate Rule of Subtraction.

"*Deduct from every Federal number twice its actual amount.* Thus: a Federal scouting party captures 100 Confederates. From this 100 you must deduct 200, which leaves a balance of 100 in our favor; and instead of the Yankees getting 100 Confederates, the Confederates get 100 Yankees. It was by this rule that Gen. Bragg defeated Rosecrans.

"Thus, Sweet Idiot," I said, "I have explained to you those great fundamental laws of mathematics which underlie the Confederacy; and I am the Confederate Archimedes, he who was equally skilled in astronomy, geometry, mechanics, hydrostatics, and optics, in all of which he excelled, and produced many extraordinary inventions; but, in my opinion, notwithstanding his miraculous skill as displayed in the defense of Syracuse, he never conceived an idea so grand as the Confederate Arithmetic."

Yours, mathematically,

JAMES B. MACPHERSON.

CHAPTER X.

HYMN OF SALVATION.

BY JAMES R. MACPHERSON,
Poet Laureate of Madisonville.

SMITE and slay the savage Yankee!
  Break and pulverise his bones!
It is done; and I will thank thee,
  Great Confederate Paul Jones!*

Lo! E. Pluribus and Unum
  Now are rolling in the dirt!
Bravo Confederate, who hast hewn 'em,
  Rise and put on a clean shirt!

Now the Pelican is flopping
  His broad wings in feather high;
On, Confederacy! no stopping—
  Every Yankee Dog shall die!

Never more an EXTRA ERA
  Shall announce a blown-up Queen;*
Oh, P. Jones, you are my deary,
  And the biggest brick I've seen!

Light is breaking from the heaven!
  Yea, it streams athwart the sky!
I myself can slay eleven—
  Every Yankee Dog shall die!

Now Orleans has been delivered!
  Do you ask the reason why?
Fate's designs shall be uncovered—
  Every Yankee Dog shall die!

"Queen of the West," a vessel captured by the rebels, after
having run the Vicksburg batteries, and destroyed during the campaign of General Banks up the Teche, in the spring of 1863. She
was commanded by Fuller, who aspired to the title of the Confederate Paul Jones!

CHAPTER XI.

MACPHERSON DEDICATES HIMSELF TO WAR AND LARCENY.—
HE ENCOUNTERS THE HONEST JEW.

LOUISIANA LOWLANDS LOW,
April 25th, 1803.

SIR:—For some time rumors of the most painful
nature reached my ears, while, in my dilapidated hospitable abode at Madisonville, I was preparing my
mind to offer my life in the sacred cause of the Confederacy. I read in THE ERA that Gen. Banks had
advanced from Brashear City with a large force of Hessians, and that the blessed sons of the Confederacy had
been whipped, their gunboats destroyed, and their
transports captured or sunk, while they were running
before the vile Yankee foe or falling into the hands of
Ibid. But I did not believe it. I swore it could not
be true; for with that sublime faith in the Confederacy
which leads our people to receive Confederate currency
and to set facts at defiance, I scorned these statements
as Yankee inventions and falsehoods. I knew that I
was the only contributor for THE ERA who dared to
speak the truth, and blow the Confederate trumpet,
and so long as the *True Delta* and the *Picayune* had
not a word to say on the subject, which they hadn't
for many days, I possessed my sublime soul in Confederate patience, and clothed and fortified my serene
mind with stoical Confederate disbelief in every word
uttered by a Yankee.

But on Wednesday last I was aroused from my dream of security and Confederate bliss, when the *Picayune*, a paper in which I have full faith, broke the long and pleasing silence that had sealed its lips, and made known to me that there was at least some foundation for the diabolical reports in THE ERA which had appeared from time to time a week or ten days before.

Then it was that, resting my teeth upon the leg of a chair, I gave myself up to momentous meditations. Before my mind arose the incredible vision of Confederates flying before Yankees, and I cried aloud: "Ignoble, debased villain that I am!— why sit I here while my countrymen starve and run leaving their bones behind them to bleach upon the bloody field of carnage, and while one of the children of my loins languishes in a loathsome dungeon in Baronne street? Arise, Macpherson! abandon the seductive paths of philosophy and poetry, buckle on a C. S. plate, shoulder a double-barrelled shot-gun, and plunge headlong into the deep-flowing tide of Yankee homicide and larceny!"

I then arose in my terrible might, while my dilapidated hospitable abode trembled to the top of the stove-pipe beneath the massive heel of my new boots, with which I smote the quaking ground; and I swore by the mud image of Jeff. Davis, which had just been set up by my Idiotic Boy, that I never would wash my face or taste a drop of water until I had exterminated every Yankee, man, woman, and child, in the States of Louisiana, Mississippi, Arkansas, and the First Congressional District of Texas!

"Not drink any water, James!" exclaimed my wife, in a tone of astonishment; "what will you drink?"

" Rum !" I answered, with a voice like bellowing thunder; "rum, my love! and rum alone !"

Therefore I dedicated myself to the god of war: " O Mars !" I exclaimed, " the fatherless son of Juno, whose delight was in contest and strife, and who wast a warrior of severe countenance, with a cuirass and an Argive shield upon thine arm! —thee I invoke, and to thee I dedicate my vast and comprehensive intellect, and the death-compassing stroke of my unapproachable arm !" I then went forth on my mission of destruction, breathing revenge and blood from my nostrils at every step.

The Honest Jew.

Just after crossing the Yankee lines, I encountered an individual who informed me that he was an Honest Jew. "Right glad am I to meet you, my noble friend," I said: "for honest men are scarce in these unwholesome days. I trust you are an Israelite in whom there is no guile."

" I ish dat," responded the Honest Jew; "and vat I say, dat pe trute."

" Then," I answered, "you are a good Confederate ; for Confederates alone are capable of speaking the truth."

" You vait vun little pit," returned the guileless Israelite, "an' I show you I make seventeen hunder tollar in fifteen minutes !"

" How ?" I asked.

" I shut up Yankee's eye."

The Honest Jew then beckoned me to follow him. Approaching the Yankee sentinel, he said:

"I habe tree hunder tollar goods back yonder. I take 'em across that bayou I get two tousan'. Now you must shut your eye vile I goes py, an' I gives you fifty tollar!"

"All right," replied the Yankee sentinel, "give me the $50 and I'll shut my eye while you pass."

The Honest Jew paid the Yankee the sum specified, and the Jew went back after his goods. But I noticed that the sentinel called the corporal of the guard and had some private conversation with him, after which the corporal disappeared.

Soon the Jew came up with his goods, and the Yankee sentinel didn't see him at all when he passed; but he hadn't got fifty yards before the corporal and four men dodged out from behind a tree and arrested him. His goods were seized and confiscated, and he was told that if he ever tried such a dodge again, he would be sent to Fort Jackson with a ball and chain to his leg.

"Var's mine fifty tollar?" said the Honest Jew, shaking his fist at the Yankee sentinel.

"I have it," replied the base Yankee dog; "you gave it to me to shut my eyes while you passed, and I fulfilled my part of the bargain."*

I then resumed my journey to New Orleans, accompanied by the Israelite in whom there was no guile, and whose deep-heaving sighs and groans of agony over his loss, touched me with pity, and filled my mind with tenfold anger against the foul despotism of the United States.

* A true incident. ED.

"My guileless and honest friend," I said to him, "you are a victim of unmitigated villany and iron oppression. You would do good by supplying the Confederacy and getting rich at the same time; but the damnable and debased despotism of the United States steps in your way!"

"Oh, I pe very boor—very boor, indeed!" groaned the Israelite in whom there was no guile.

"My boor friend!" I exclaimed, clasping him to my bosom, "I will avenge thy manifold wrongs. I have dedicated myself to Mars, the death-scattering hero of bloody wars; and now I also dedicate myself to Hermes, the god of thieves, and the son of Jupiter and Maia; he whose first act was to steal the cattle of Apollo. Henceforth, I am the champion of larceny, and I swear by the soul of the Confederacy, that I will not rest from toil and labor until I have stolen a horse!"

"You gives him to me, eh?" asked the Jew, his eyes lighting up with eager fire.

"Yes," I replied, "I'll give him to thee, my wronged and outraged friend."

"But tree horses only make me cood for mine coods."

"Then three shalt thou have" I exclaimed. "Yes, I swear it by the honor of a Confederate Warrior, that I will steal three horses for this outraged Jew, and one for myself, before I consent to a cessation of hostilities, or return to the pursuits of philosophy in Madisonville"

The Honest Jew pressed me to his bosom as we parted in New Orleans, and promised to wait at the

Opelousas Depot, in Algiers, until I should send him the three horses.

Successful Scheme of Finance.

It was about this time that I put into practical operation a great scheme of finance that I had studied out in my secluded and meditative hours, in my dilapidated hospitable abode at Madisonville, and I found that it worked to perfection. The principle is as follows: Never invite a man to drink, but always drink when you are asked. By the application of this simple rule, you get for your own use all the liquor you pay for, and also get a good deal which doesn't cost you any thing.

I crossed the river on the Canal-street ferry-boat, with the firm determination not to pay a cent for food, lodging, or transportation, during my travels. Since then I have passed through many scenes, which it will require a long letter to describe, and I hereby give notice to the public that my Twelfth Epistle will be devoted to a full and authentic account of my travels in the Louisiana Lowlands Low, and to a description of the many strange adventures I have encountered.

Yours unremittingly,

JAMES B. MACPHERSON.

CHAPTER XII.

The Great Confederate Traveller describes his Journey through the Louisiana Lowlands Low.

Note.—Algiers is the name of a small town opposite New Orleans. It contains the depot of the Opelousas railroad. Ferry accommodations are miserable. At the time this letter was written, General Banks's brilliant campaign through the Teche country was in progress, and had already resulted in the destruction of the rebel army of Western Louisiana. Two thousand prisoners had been captured, and a considerable number of them had been confined in the Belleville Iron Works in Algiers, which led Mr. Macpherson to suppose that the building was in possession of the Confederates.——The rebel army which was so effectually dispersed or destroyed by the movement of General Banks, was in command of Gen. Richard Taylor, a son of "Old Zack," the hero and patriot, whose devotion to his country has rendered his name dear to every true American. As Gen. Banks's campaign through the Teche country seems not to have been generally understood at the time, the author will briefly give what he supposes to have been the theory of the movement. "Why," it was asked, "should the United States forces march through a country, take possession of it, and forthwith abandon it, leaving the inhabitants who, expecting protection, had shown a love for the Union, to suffer the penalty of rebel vengeance? This would be a pertinent inquiry under ordinary circumstances, but the author believes a brief statement of facts will explain this matter to the satisfaction of every impartial reader.

The great object which General Banks must have had in view, was the capture of Port Hudson and the opening of the Mississippi river. But Port Hudson was a hundred and fifty miles above New Orleans, and in order to invest it successfully, the General required every soldier in the department. Indeed, with every soldier, his force was seemingly inadequate to the undertaking. The rebel garrison of Port Hudson, at the time of its investment, in May, 1863, numbered seven thousand effective men, and at no time during the siege did Gen. Banks command more than ten thousand effective men. His lines were necessarily much longer than those of the enemy, and the advantages were all with the garrison, except in the matter of sup plies. In order to besiege Port Hudson, then, with any prospect of success, it was necessary that he should take every available man that could be spared. But Taylor, Mouton, and Sibley were in Western Louisiana with a large force of rebels, and if he moved his entire army to Port Hudson, he left his rear and New Orleans itself exposed to the enemy. As he had not a sufficient force to watch the enemy in Western Louisiana and to invest Port Hudson at the same time, it was necessary to destroy the rebel army of Western Louisiana before Port Hudson could be invested. And this work was most successfully accomplished. The Army of the Gulf accomplished a march of three hundred miles in twenty days, fighting four battles and winning as many victories. The first battle was at Camp Bisland, christened after a planter by that name, whose plantation, now a picture of ruin and desolation, is situated on the Teche, between Berwick City and the village of Franklin. The rebel army of Western Louisiana was completely broken up and destroyed by the campaign; and having accomplished this indispensable preliminary step, Gen. Banks at once moved his whole force against Port Hudson. Such, the author believes, was the theory of the Teche campaign—a campaign which, in rapidity of movement, in general management and important results, has not been surpassed in the history of this war, if we take into account the number of men engaged.

Brashear City (why will people call such insignificant places cities?) is situated on Berwick Bay, near the confluence of the Teche and Atchafalaya rivers. It was the base of supplies in the Teche campaign, and the more recent movement by which the rebel army was drawn out of Texas, opening the way for the success of the expedition to the Rio Grande. The place was recaptured by the rebels in June, 1863, almost without resistance by our forces; and large quantities of stores, ammunition, and a considerable number of prisoners, fell into the hands of the enemy. After the fall of Port Hudson, however, the rebels hastily evacuated the place, and just in time to escape capture. It is about ninety miles from New Orleans to the westward, and the Opelousas Railroad has its present termini at Algiers and Brashear City. The country between the two places is very low, and wide forests are seen on either hand. There are plenty of alligators to be seen sunning themselves, and some are of enormous size; although it requires the Confederate arithmetic to make them five hundred feet long, as has been done by Mr. Macpherson.——The author made the journey described in the following letter (i. e. as far as Brashear City), in the latter part of April, for the first time; and his experience at the Brashear City Hotel can only be appreciated by those who have visited "the Great Temple of Wisdom."——He has connected the philosophy of Macpherson with the ancient mythology, ·

because the credulity, mendacity, passions, and habits of the secessionists more properly belong to the religion of a pagan country than to a land and an age of civilisation. Gov. Moore, the last Chief Magistrate elected by the people of Louisiana, and his itinerant Legislature still claiming to exercise executive and legislative functions, were frightened by the "Yankee" army, or the expectation of its approach, and "skedaddled" to some indefinite point, in or beyond the extreme western portion of Louisiana. Moore still claims to be governor of Louisiana. His power is about equal to that of Sancho Panza, who, like Moore, also gloried in the title of "Governor."

MADISONVILLE, LA.,
May 2, 1863.

Sir:—As Ulysses, the much planning warrior of the Greeks, wandered the victim of cruel Fate, searching vainly for his home, whence he sighed to return victorious from the siege of Troy, even so was I driven from the paths of philosophy, and from my dilapidated hospitable abode, by the articulate-speaking voice of Fate, which sent me forth the great Confederate Traveller in the Louisiana Lowlands Low.

Taking passage on one of those magnificent steamers belonging to the Canal street Ferry, that are fitted up on a scale of magnificence surpassing the dreams of Fairy Land, or the splendor and glory which surround the President of the Confederacy in his stately and oriental palace at Richmond, I stood upon the lofty deck and thus poured out my soul to the people of New Orleans: "Farewell," I cried in tearful tones, "fair Crescent City, gazing upon the great old Father of Waters! thee I leave behind. But when I return, I shall come with banner, brand, and bow, leading the victorious and unconquerable legions of Gen. R. Taylor, and exterminating the vile Yankee foe, whose iron foot rests upon the bosom of the Confederacy, with terrible weight, as the great Polyphemus, the one-eyed Giant, thirsting for human life, had plucked a woolly mountain from its base and placed it on my head!" I then shouted three times, and committed assault and battery on a newsboy who offered me THE ERA.

Arriving at Algiers, a magnificent city opposite New Orleans, I discovered that the Belleville Iron Works had fallen into the possession of the Confederacy, and that it contained a strong garrison of Graybacks, numbering several hundred. "Blessed be Jupiter," I exclaimed, "the Father of gods and men, and the overshadowing ruler of cloudy Olympus!—for now I perceive that the invader of the Lowlands Low has been driven back with terrific slaughter!" I then sent a dispatch to the President of the Confederacy in Richmond, announcing that General Banks had been defeated and completely wiped out; that General R. Taylor had captured eighteen hundred thousand Yankee prisoners, and that the head of his invincible column was then in the Belleville Iron Works of Algiers, protected and watched over by a strong line of Yankee sentinels.

I then went to the Yankee Railroad Depot, and demanded a free pass to Brashear City.

"By what authority," inquired the Yankee, "do you make that demand?"

"By the authority of the Southern Confederacy," I replied, "and in virtue of my vow to Mars, the death-scattering hero of bloody wars, that I will neither wash my face nor drink water until I have exterminated every damned Yankee in Louisiana, Mississippi, and the First Congressional District of Texas!"

"You must be Macpherson," replied the Yankee.

"Well and truly hast thou spoken," I answered him;

"I AM Macpherson, the great Confederate traveller, whose Massive Intellect will produce a volume of Travels more entertaining, though less truthful, than the tales of the Arabian Nights."

"If that won't pass you over this road," answered the Yankee, "I don't know what will." He then gave me a dead-head ticket and introduced me to another chap, who at once made me drink a bottle of champagne, after which I started off on my journey.

"Now, indeed," I exclaimed, "is the will of Jupiter made manifest, and heaven sends auspicious omens; for I ride at the expense of the United States, and am drunk to start with, without cost—the indispensable condition of a Confederate Traveller and Warrior."

"Why is it," asked a chap in the cars, "that you still adhere to the religion of the Greeks and Romans, believe in omens, and offer orisons to the divinities of Olympus, whose worship has been overthrown by the light of Christianity?"

"Untaught Ignoramus!" I answered; "benighted heathen of Yankee darkness! if thy dull brain is capable of comprehending the Confederate principles, I will explain them to you. The Confederate religion is a conglomeration of the faith of Moses and the intellectual fables of Olympus, which have been handed down to us by the greatest poets of the earth. As the Jews believe they are the chosen people, and a cussed sight better than anybody else, so do the Confederates believe that they are the salt of the earth—a position fully sustained by the large saline deposits near New Iberia. So far, then, our faith is founded on Moses and the Israelites generally; but the rest of it corre-

sponds pretty faithfully with the pagan religion, except
that ours surpasses the pagan in the magnificent splendor of its fables. Let me illustrate this point to your
ignorance-besotted mind. Ancient Troy was a village
about half the size of Algiers, and the siege of the
place was a series of fist-encounters between Ajax,
Heenan, Priam, and other prize-fighters. But Homer
has converted his pugilists into demigods, and has introduced nearly all the gods of heaven, earth, and hell
as interested spectators, or active co-operationists. For
all this there was a slight foundation in truth ; and the
Confederate Religion differs from and surpasses the
ancient, in the fact that its biggest stories and achieve-
ments have no foundation in fact whatever!" I then
presented him with a copy of Macpherson's Confederate Arithmetic, and told him that if his muddy and
debased brain could comprehend it, he was smarter
than I was.

The people along the road turned out by millions to
see me, as the train passed on through the Lowlands
Low, all giving a hundred and fifty cheers and fifty
tigers, in honor of the Plato of the Confederacy and
the Venus of Madisonville, whose Mammoth Brain
first brought together in a condensed and intelligible
form the famous religion and philosophy of the New
Nation, which are destined to sweep every other from
the earth, from Greenland's Icy Mountains to India's
Coral Strand:

The car in which I was seated was soon filled with
bonquets, hurled at me through the window, formed
of red, white, and red, indicative of the Confederate
flag, and in imitation of those which the Confederates

of New Orleans have been accustomed to throw at the players, since the damnable despotism of U. S. will not permit them to throw out-and-out secession flags. At last, the accumulated weight of bouquets and of my Ponderous Intellect proved too much for the laboring Engine, and it gave out, when we were kept waiting for three hours, surrounded by impenetrable woods and dirty water, moccasin snakes and deep lagoons, overhung by weeping cypress-trees, and echoing forever with the melodious notes of bull-frogs and alligators.

Then it was that I walked into the gloomy forest, and recalled to my mind the adventure of Balboa, who discovered the Pacific Ocean, and wading into it up to his waist, stretched forth his sword and took possession of that important stream in the name of his king. Therefore I waded into a mud-hole up to the top of my breeches, and stretching forth my brawny arm, took possession of it in the name of the Southern Confederacy!

Macpherson's Interview with an Alligator five hundred feet long.

As I was wallowing back, I met an alligator five hundred feet long by Confederate measurement, which is equal to ten feet in Yankee mathematics. I immediately drew my Jeff. Davis revolver, a terrible brass-mounted weapon, presented to me by the ladies of Doctor Palmer's congregation, and shot the animal, expecting to see him die at my feet. He paid no attention to it, but rolled over in the dirt and yawned, as though nothing had happened. Then it was that my mind

5

was filled with admiration and love for the noble animal, to whom I delivered the following able address: "Majestic Confederate mudsill!—aboriginal inhabitant of the Louisiana Lowlands Low!—thou art impregnable as the defenses of Camp Bisland, and impervious to water and mud alike. Would to heaven that, deployed as skirmishers in R. Taylor's army, you might wade in Yankee blood, even as now you wallow in mud, the natural ally of the Southern Confederacy!"

Arrival at Tigerville.

The engine having been repaired, it gave a Confederate snort, and with lightning in its eye and steel in its sinews, drew us to Tigerville, just as the sombre mantle of all-enshrouding night settled over the earth. The conductor shouted "Tigerville," and I looked out, expecting to see a city equal to Madisonville, but could discover nothing but a wide and lonely forest, in which the deep-laid shadows seemed to conceal a thousand phantom forms. But as the train moved on again, I got a sight at Tigerville, which apparently consisted of a grocery store and a brass kettle; and I found that by a miraculous junction of nature and art, while the engine was in the centre of the city, the rear car, in which I was seated, was in the midst of primeval forests, stretching away for miles on either hand.

At last we reached Brashear City, a town larger than New Orleans, if you include the woods. A peculiarity of this city is, that it has no streets.

The great Temple of Wisdom at Brashear City.

Immediately I proceeded to the Brashear City Hotel, which I soon discovered was a vast temple of wisdom and economy. It so strongly resembles my dilapidated hospitable abode in Madisonville, that I burst into tears as the sweet image of that home arose before me with the Idiotic Boy, now the exponent of Confederate Philosophy, and of my spouse, who sighs for the return of her roving protector, even as Penelope sighed for the return of Ulysses; but I hope she has fewer suitors than the excellent Greek lady alluded to.

Calling for supper, I was told that none could be had; as it was past the usual hour, and the chief cook had gone to bed. Then was I filled with admiration at the Arcadian simplicity of life in those remote regions, where the repose of a cook begins at nine o'clock in the evening, and is guarded by the changeless law of custom. Gladly, therefore, did I go to my room, supperless.

The apartment in which I was placed, and from which a Yankee was expelled to make room for me, filled me with love and admiration beyond the power of language to describe. There was such an absence of all luxuries, or even necessaries of life, that I at once saw that the architect and proprietor of the establishment was a philosopher and a political economist. The rude walls were constructed of rough Confederate boards, undefiled by the carpenter's plane, the luxurious covering of the paper manufactory, or the unnecessary embellishment of the white-washer's brush.

"Thanks to Jupiter!" I exclaimed, "the wall-paper which might otherwise have been wasted upon these walls, can now be used for publishing secession journals." I then got into bed, and pulled down the musquito-net. I discovered that the mattress was made of cane-stalks, the products of my native Louisiana, with an immense one in the centre, very convenient to hang upon to keep one's self in bed. The only unnecessary luxury I observed consisted of two table-cloths on the bed in place of sheets; and I got up early in the morning, thinking they might be needed for use on the table. I had not been in bed a great while before the musquitoes, that were buzzing by millions around the net, commenced pouring through in close column by battalions; while an immense force was held back as a reserve to fill up the ranks shattered by the death-scattering blows of my manly arm. Now it was that a great physical rencounter commenced, surpassing in bloody destruction the battle of Forts Jackson and St. Philip. I slaughtered them without mercy; but I found that the wide forests surrounding the city were filled with dauntless legions; and however many millions I might destroy, it was probable that I should be compelled at last to surrender to overpowering numbers. Therefore, I thought I would try to stop up some of the holes in the musquito-net. I stuck my hat into one of them, my boots into two others, my breeches into another, my Confederate coat and vest into another, and finally, the washstand and pitcher into the biggest one. But these precautions scarcely checked the overpowering advance of the hostile armies, and I went to tying up the holes in knots, until I had tied twenty-five hundred by the Confederate arithmetic, which is fifty in Yankee mathematics; but all to no avail. I at last collected the carcasses of the slain, and piled them up around me; after which I was enabled to enjoy a night of strength-nourishing repose.

Arising in the morning, I discovered that there was no soap in the room, which I regarded as a high personal compliment to my cleanliness; it was as much as an admission on the part of the landlord, that I was clean enough already. Neither was there any looking-glass; and I knew at once that the landlord did not mean to encourage the sentiments of worldly pride, engendered in men and women when they survey their persons in a glass.

I immediately took passage for Opelousas, whence I walked to Shreveport to find Governor Moore and the Legislature, the custodians of the civil rights of Louisiana, and the guardians of the State treasury.

Interview with Governor Moore.

I inquired diligently for them, but the inhabitants reported that they had left some time previous, at double-quick, carrying the treasury and archives in a one-horse cart. I followed on and reached the Red River; and there I discovered Governor Moore weeping on a stump, in the depths of a dismal forest, surrounded by insects and wild beasts. Seeing me, he fell upon my neck and cried like a child. "Guardian of law and order!" I exclaimed; "protector of States' rights and the treasury, dauntless commander-in-chief of the

State militia! thee do I embrace in fraternal and undying Confederate affection. Tell me, I pray thee, the
cause of thine overwhelming grief."

"Macpherson!" he said, in tearful tones; "look
here on this picture, and then on this. When I took
charge of the Legislature, it sat in the fine State-house
at Baton Rouge, and I was the proud potentate of the
great sugar-planting State, while the treasury was
overflowing with funds. But where am I now?"

"In a swamp, on a stump!" I replied.

"Where is the treasury?" he continued.

"That's what I'm after," I answered.

"Well, thou shalt see it," he replied; whereupon he
led me to the borders of a mud-hole, and drawing aside
the thick overhanging foliage, displayed to my vision
a one-horse cart attached to a mule, and both stuck in
the mud. "To this complexion hath it come at last!"
he groaned; "for you see before you the archives and
the treasury of the State!"

I immediately overhauled the contents, and discovered the Act of Secession, of January 26, 1861; a copy
of Macpherson's Confederate Arithmetic, by which he
had tried to multiply 0 by 50, and so fill the treasury;
and an order conscripting all able-bodied niggers into
the Confederate ranks as soldiers. "Those," said the
Itinerant Moore, "are the State archives. Look now
at the treasury." I looked, and discovered a five-cent
shinplaster on the bank of West Baton Rouge, a blue
car-ticket, and a receipt for two barrels of whisky.
"That," said the weeping Moore, "is what remains of
the wealth of Louisiana, after passing through the fiery
ordeal of civil war, and the more trying ordeal of my

policy. The mule represents the motive power of the Confederacy, and the whole concern is now stuck in the mud."

"But the glory of the New Nation still remains," I answered him. "Jeff. Davis still sits enthroned in oriental magnificence in Richmond, and the Idiotic Boy is monarch of Confederate Philosophy. Let us arise and exterminate the Yankee race!"

We arose, and taking me to the recesses of an immense hollow tree, I discovered the Legislature in session. It consisted of three members, all dead drunk. "Join us," said the governor; and I joined. We soon became happy in the consciousness that we might soon recover the whole territory of the United States. I was accordingly elected a member of the Legislature, and we forthwith passed an act declaring the power of the Yankees at an end, and seizing the whole continent of America, in the name of the Southern Confederacy, the said act to take effect immediately. "Thanks to Jupiter!" I exclaimed; "the war is now at an end; the North is subdued, and the flag of the New Nation floats in triumph over every inch of ground on the vast continent." We then got blind drunk, from which I was aroused by the recollection that a week before I had made a vow of larceny, and had promised to steal three horses for the Honest Jew, who had promised to wait in Algiers until I should send him the specified number of animals. I accordingly started off at double-quick, and returned to the Yankee headquarters at Opelousas.

The Vow of Larceny fulfilled.

I was there advised that the late battle-field of Camp
Bisland afforded great facilities for stealing horses, and
thither I went. Looking around, I discovered not less
than sixty animals, and I immediately telegraphed to
the Honest Jew, that if ho would come up there, I
would give him thirty horses instead of three. He
went and met me with a glowing face on that field of
bloody encounter, in which R. Taylor's forces drove
the Yankees thirteen hundred miles in thirteen hours,
averaging a hundred miles to the hour. He immediately embraced me.

"You pe van shentlemans," said he; " I bays your
pills at the hotel."

"All right," I answered him; "there are sixty
horses up there; you shall have thirty; take your
pick."

He started off on the run, but soon returned with
fire and indignation in his eyes.

"You pe van tam fillain!" he exclaimed.

"What's the matter, sweet one!" I asked, in a tone
of tenderness.

"You tam fillain! the horses pe every vun tend!"

"Dead!" I exclaimed, "and so young—the oldest
not being quite twenty! But weep not, my Honest
Jew; they died in the sacred cause of the Southern
Confederacy. *Dulce et decorum est pro patriâ mori.*
You never tried it, poor Jew, and you never will.
But, I tell thee, I did not promise that the horses
should be alive; and now, O Hermes! god of thieves,

I have fulfilled my vow of blood and larceny!" I
then kissed the Honest Jew and returned to New Orleans, having been invited to preach in a secession
church on Sunday, April 26th, in consequence of my
able exposition of the Confederate Religion to the
Yankee Ignoramus, and in view of the fact that the
proclamation of that bloody despot, Abraham Lincoln,
had been ordered to be read in the churches on that
day. The prevailing belief among the Confederates
was, that I was the only Confederate parson smart
enough to do the thing up properly, and outwit the
dull Yankee brain. Therefore did I haste, with wings
as swift as meditation or the thoughts of love, to assume the robes of divinity. In my next letter, I shall
appear as the Great Confederate Parson, reading the
Proclamation, and will reproduce the sermon I delivered on that occasion.

My task for this week is done. I travelled through
the Louisiana Lowlands Low, with a rapidity that
would do credit to an engine on the Opelousas road.
I am the greatest traveller in the Confederacy, and my
only wonder is that my heart does not swell with pride
and egotism when I think of my accomplishments.
But with all my Massive Intellect and power in the
Confederacy, I am not egotistic in any degree beyond
what is warranted in the Confederate Code of Egotism.

Yours, modestly,

JAMES B. MACPHERSON.

5*

CHAPTER XIII.

MACPHERSON APPEARS AS A CLERGYMAN, AND EXPOUNDS THE
CONFEDERATE GOSPEL.—HE ENCOUNTERS THE WEEPING
ORPHAN, AND UNEXPECTEDLY FINDS A LARGE FAMILY ON
HIS HANDS.—HE PREACHES FROM THE TEXT: "BLOW YE!"
ETC., ETC.

NOTE.—President Lincoln issued a proclamation, setting apart the
30th day of April, 1863, as a day of national humiliation, fasting, and
prayer. General James Bowen, Provost Marshal General of Louisiana,
issued a circular, in which he "requested" (that was the word used)
all the clergymen officiating in the churches of New Orleans, Jefferson, Carrolton, and Algiers, to read the proclamation of the President
to their congregations, on Sunday, the 26th of April—the Sunday pre-
ceding the day designated by the President. Some of the clergymen
paid no attention to this request. Others read it, and the reading
was made the occasion for very noisy and disgraceful demonstrations
on the part of the secessionists in the congregation. The women
took the lead in the sacrilegious proceedings. The moment the reading commenced, they left the churches in a very noisy and offensive
manner, shuffling their feet, upsetting stools, and otherwise disturb-
ing the peace and good order of the sanctuary. Some of the clergymen, anxious to soothe the nerves of their secession hearers, announced that they would read the Proclamation because they had
been *ordered* to read it—an assertion as false as it was cowardly,
since, as has been stated already, they were only *requested* to read it.
One of the clergy who neglected to read it at all was Father Joubert,
of St. Augustine's church, who, the author has been told, refused to
administer the sacrament to colored men who had enlisted in the
army; thus making it an offense punishable with eternal damnation
for a negro to fight for the Union! Father Lemaitre, of the St. Rose
de Lima, read the proclamation, and preached an out-and-out Union
sermon to an immense congregation. He was soon after excommu-
nicated by Archbishop Odin; but the author is pleased to learn that
he paid no attention to his sentence, refused to be damned in all his
parts for the sin of being a Union man, and still continues to exercise his ecclesiastical office. One clergyman, whose congregation un-

dersood only the French language, read the proclamation in English; which would seem to warrant Macpherson in reading it in the Æthiopic.

MADISONVILLE, LA.,
May 9, 1863.

SIR:—I am greater than Hercules, the son of Jupiter, for he performed but twelve labors of immortal distinction; but I, having performed twelve, now enter upon my thirteenth with my Mammoth Brain undimmed, and the fires of genius glowing more brightly than when I began.

Returning from my immortal travels through the Louisiana Lowlands Low, I had scarcely set foot upon the Levee at New Orleans, when a courier, mounted on a Confederate mule, came riding up with the rapidity of lightning. "I am," he said, "the bearer of important dispatches from your Idiotic Boy, the Great exponent of Confederate Philosophy in Madisonville, since your departure from your dilapidated hospitable abode."

I opened the dispatches with a trembling hand, and was startled at the vast importance of the matter therein contained. Jeff. Davis, whose mud image stands upon my shelf in Madisonville, and which I always approach with uncovered head, had telegraphed to the Idiotic Boy as follows:

Jeff. Davis's Dispatch.

The Proclamation of Abraham Lincoln appointing a day of national humiliation and prayer, must not be read in the churches of New Orleans; or, if read, it must be received with hisses, howls, and Confederate

snorts. Your father, James B. Macpherson, is charged
with the execution of this order.

> I am, my dear Idiot,
>> Your faithful imitator,
>>> JEFF. DAVIS,
>>>> President of the
>>>> American Continent.

"Thanks to Jupiter!" I exclaimed, "the son and
conqueror of Saturn, whose thunders resound from
Olympus like the roar of a Confederate shot-gun ; it is
my pleasant duty and province to stay the tide of
Yankee sacrilege, and save from defilement the great
Confederate Temple of Holiness!" I then looked at
the town-clock to see what time it was, and found
that it was precisely six P. M.

As I was gazing upon the clock, whose massive
hands mark the rapid departure of the fleet-footed
hours, I was tapped upon the shoulder by a man of
giant frame. His form towered on high more lofty
than that of the bloody despot Abraham Lincoln,
whose throne at Washington is built of human skulls,
and whose daily food is a fricasseed Southerner. His
large and glowing face was red as a Confederate army
shoe, and his threadbare gray garments showed me
plainly that he belonged to the glorious New Nation.
He gazed upon me with a look of melting tenderness
with those fiery eyes, beaming in their sunken sockets
like the orbs of night, or the all-warming sun in his
meridian glory, and falling at my knees, he burst into
a flood of tears.

"I am a Weeping Orphan!" he said: "I am six

feet and five inches high, and forty-nine years of age. Weight, two hundred and eighty pounds."

"Unhappy youth!" I exclaimed: "thine enormous height entitles thee to the sympathy of a Confederate philosopher, even if thou, tender bud and sweet honey-suckle of affliction, hadst not been cast upon the cold charities of the world at a tender age."

"How do you make that out?" asked a Yankee, in a gruff voice, interrupting my train of sublime meditation; "up North we call a man of forty-nine years well advanced in life!"

"And so he is," I answered, "in those unhappy realms of Yankeedom; but in the celestial Confederacy a man does not arrive at the years of discretion until he is fifty-one." I then fell upon the breast of the Weeping Orphan, and told him that I would share with him my last crust, and invited him to my quarters at the St. Louis Hotel, which invitation he accepted with flowing tears of gratitude.

Macpherson finds himself with a large family on his hands.

Scarcely had we taken four drinks, before the Orphan burst into a flood of such violent tears that I feared the effect upon his tender constitution. "Oh!" he cried, "what will become of those sweet buds of affection, my wailing infants, who groan for bread; and my tender spouse, whose grief surpasses my own?"

"Bring them hither," I exclaimed; "I will protect them from the cold blasts of the world, and fill their mouths with bread and jerked beef."

"Generous stranger!" exclaimed the Orphan; "I accept the proffered hospitalities of your house." He then brought in his family, which consisted of a wife and thirteen children, and all about the same size. "These are the cause of my anxiety," he exclaimed, "and for these I weep almost as much as for my own bereaved lot, cast as I am, at a tender age, upon my own resources."

"I will keep this charge!" I answered, "and thou shalt know that none ever in vain appealed to the charity of the Plato of the Confederacy." I then ordered supper for the crowd, and found that it would cost me $85 per day to feed my unhappy guests.

Sunday morning, April 26, 1863, dawned upon the world with resplendent glory. The all-beholding sun shone from a cloudless sky, and the birds sang sweetly around the lofty chimneys of the St. Louis Hotel, where I might have been seen arm-in-arm with the Weeping Orphan, followed by his wife and thirteen infants, wending our way towards the Great Confederate Temple of Holiness, in Camp-street. The people, attracted by the understanding that I was to expound the Confederate religion, and read Abraham Lincoln's Proclamation in a Confederate manner, turned out in overpowering numbers. At least three hundred thousand registered enemies were present, and as many more went away, unable to gain admittance.

Not having a pastoral robe I pulled off my coat, and mounted the pulpit in my shirt sleeves, where I was received with loud applause. The women waved their handkerchiefs and cried, "God bless you!" I was always popular with the women of New Orleans, and the reason of it is that I so profusely and ably represent their thoughts, feelings, and wishes. I am endowed with the extraordinary gift of nature, which enables me to read the innermost emotions and thoughts of the human mind. I comprehend to its fullest extent that deep, and intense, and passionate, and divine super-human hatred, which the true ladies of New Orleans cherish in their glowing bosoms for the whole Yankee race—a hatred as deep as the twelfth circle of Dante's Inferno, and as high as the flag-staff of the St. Charles Hotel before it was cut down. Hate the Yankees? Yes! I hate thirst, when there is no Confederate rum within a hundred miles of me! I had rather be a door-keeper in a Confederate hog-pen than to play a piano in the parlor of a Yankee. Therefore it is that I am popular with the true ladies of New Orleans; and therefore it is, that the moment I stepped into the pulpit I was loaded down with bouquets and sympathy.

The audience began to cry out, "Macpherson! Macpherson!" I was about to respond, when, much to my astonishment and indignation, the Weeping Orphan dodged in ahead of me, and with streaming eyes informed the people of his unhappy lot in life. It occurred to me that something might be made out of the affair: I proposed that a collection should be taken up for the weeping object of sympathy before me. Three thousand dollars were collected, which I put in my own pocket, and then proceeded with the exercises.

"Confederate saints," I said, "and believers in the only true faith, we shall begin this performance by singing a beautiful hymn, composed by myself, and touchingly appropriate to the mournful occasion on which we meet."

YANKEES.

Hymn in L. M., by Rev. JAMES B. MACPHERSON, of Madisonville, Poet Laureate, Author, Philosopher, Warrior, and Traveller.

1.

Yankees have horns and hoofs and tails,
The soil is blighted where they tread,
And be they women, be they males,
I wish the Yankee race was dead.

2.

Confederate vengeance, like a blow
From the avenging hand of Fate,
Shall lay all the damned Yankees low
In our brave Louisiana State.

I requested the choir to omit the first and second stanzas of the above beautiful hymn, which they did. The singing concluded, I proceeded to deliver my great discourse.

Macpherson's Sermon.

"Confederate saints and ladies," I said, "my text this morning may be found somewhere, if any of you will take the trouble to look for it; but a Confederate philosopher is necessarily so much engaged in rummaging over the Classical Dictionaries and hunting up Olympian fables with which to maintain the cause of the Confederacy, that I have not had time to ascertain the exact place where it may be found. The words are these:

"'BLOW YE!'

"In the text, as it stands in the Book, I think there

is something said about a trumpet; but it is a beautiful and sublime feature of the Confederate religion,
that you can strike out any part that don't please you,
and add any thing you'd like to see there. I have
accordingly struck out from the text the words, ' the
trumpet,' and this gives us a splendid expression of the
basis of the whole Confederate establishment, and reads
simply: ' Blow Ye!' I cannot imagine how two words
could possibly be found which more fittingly express
the duty of every Confederate. I have searched the
annals of by-gone ages; I have explored every tongue,
living and dead; I have sought in the hieroglyphics of
Egypt, the euphonious language of the Greeks, the
sublime speech of the Romans, and the fiery words of
the Gauls; but nowhere have I found two words so
worthy of the obedience of every one in the Confederacy, as those I have selected for my text on this
occasion; and therefore I cry with a loud voice:
Blow Ye!

"I have endeavored to live up to this great fundamental principle of the Confederacy, and in my life to
give a touching and noisy example of the faith. I am
the great Confederate Blower, and the reason of my
fame among men is, that I blow in a more faithful
manner than the general run of Confederates, although
the average of the Confederate race is but very little
behind me. To the Confederates of New Orleans I
give the deserved and proud distinction of Blowing in a
manner perfectly satisfactory to our King, Jeff. Davis,
President of the American Continent. To you, fair
ladies, whose beauty is unsurpassed by Hebe herself, I
award the meed of supreme merit next to myself, in

living up to this great fundamental principle of Confederate faith. I defy any man with a spark of common humanity in his breast, or the faintest gleam of common sense in his muddy and idiotic brain, to mingle
with the Confederates of New Orleans, whether in
public or social life, and say that they do not faithfully
follow the divine commandment of this text. Yes,
brother saints of both sexes, the Blowing which has
been done in your city, vindicates you forever against
the foul suspicion that you meant what you said when
you took the oath of allegiance to the United States.
Continue in this grand career, and you shall win immortal honor. As for myself, whether in sickness or
in health, in victory or death, in carnage and slaughter,
or in peace and innocence, I will Blow and Blow for-
evermore. Yea, from the table of my memory I'll
wipe away all trivial fond records, all saws and books,
all forms, all pressures past, that youth and observation
copied there; and this commandment all alone shall
live within the book and volume of my brain, unmixed
with baser matter!" I then placed my hands inge-
niously over my mouth, and blew so fiercely that it
frightened the thirteen infants of the Weeping Orphan,
and they cried in concert with me, making a most
beautiful illustration of Confederate theology.

At this stage of the proceedings, a delegation entered
from Algiers, leading a small live alligator by a red
string, which he presented to me in behalf of the
Yankee Railroad men at the Algiers Depot. The head
man informed me that this beautiful animal was captured in the Louisiana Lowlands Low, and that the
captors presented him to me as a token of regard for

the noble animal; and also that they wished to know
his dimensions by Confederate measurement. I found
that according to the rules of Confederate Arithmetic,
he was seventy-five feet long, which is equal to eighteen inches by Yankee measurement. And here allow
me to say, that the Confederate Arithmetic is perfectly
simple, and if the public will pay proper attention to
its rules, they can learn to cipher as well as I can, and
I shall not then be bothered by people coming to have
me do their sums for them. Multiply every Yankee
figure by fifty, and you get the Confederate total. The
delegation then departed, and I resumed my discourse,
having sent the animal under an escort of Stuart's
cavalry, to my dilapidated hospitable abode.

"Confederate Saints!" I said, "I have now a most
loathsome and unholy duty to perform. I have been
ordered by the Provost Marshal General, under the
penalty of death, to read in your hearing a loathsome
and unholy proclamation by that most foul and unnatural despot, Abraham Lincoln, a tyrant more base
than Caligula or the princes of Central Africa. The
proclamation fixes next Thursday as a day of national
humiliation, fasting, and prayer, and I had rather give
a thousand dollars than to read it in my temple of
Confederate Holiness, provided I was allowed to take
up another collection. But my life is of great value
to the Confederacy, and the fundamental faith of the
New Nation is, that every man shall look out for his
own neck. Rather than have my able brain separated
from the gigantic frame on which it now stands, I will
read this most hateful proclamation, and I hope the
arrangements will prove effective!"

I then commenced reading the proclamation in the Æthiopian tongue, and, simultaneously with the pronunciation of the first word, the whole audience gave the Confederate snort, while a nigger fiddler struck up the *R. Taylor Gallopade*, and forty others danced a grand hoe-down in the gallery. The Weeping Orphan pinched his thirteen children until they screamed at the top of their voice, and the ladies went to upsetting stools and drumming on the pews with their fanhandles. As soon as the reading was completed, the · audience knelt and received my benediction.

Thus did I outwit the dull Yankee brain; thus did I obey the order and trample it in the dust at the same time; thus did I save the great temple of Confederate Holiness from defilement and sacrilege.

Returning from church, I indulged in liberal potations, and made the proposition to the Weeping Orphan of taking five hundred drinks in succession, and we went at it. I recollect swallowing the thirtieth, and then my Massive Brain lost a consciousness of mundane events. But when I awoke, I found that the Weeping Orphan had stolen $3,000 out of my pocket, and skedaddled, leaving his wife and thirteen children on my hands to support. Thus, in a moment, was I reduced from luxury to abject penury and degrading poverty; and my scanty earnings barely sustain the life of the helpless ones that fortune has so unexpectedly thrown under the protecting ægis of my Benevolence.

But such is the fate of all sublunary greatness. The light that streams down from the morning sun is, ere long. hidden in the shadows of all-enshrouding night. The smile that lights up the face of innocence and beauty is soon dissipated and lost in the haggard lines of grief. The step of youth must some day totter with age; the glory of life is transient as the meteor's flash; and until I have an opportunity to take up another collection, or to steal a thousand dollars, I must grapple, single-handed and alone, with the ill fortunes of life, and remain gaunt with famine and thirst.

Yours, theologically,

JAMES B. MACPHERSON.

CHAPTER XIV.

MACPHERSON AS A MILITARY CHIEFTAIN.—HE IS APPOINTED
A MAJOR GENERAL OF CONFEDERATE VOLUNTEERS.—HE
ISSUES A PROCLAMATION, RAISES AN ARMY, AND WINS
TWO BATTLES IN A SINGLE DAY, ETC., ETC.

NOTE.—The rebel forces at Pontchatoula, the capture of which
place has already been noted, were composed, in part, of Choctaw
Indians. Some of these were captured and brought to New Orleans
as prisoners of war.

MADISONVILLE, LA.,
May 10th, 1863.

SIR:—Plunged suddenly into the depths of military
glory and renown, it becomes my pleasant duty to ac-
quaint the admiring millions who read my able productions, that Jeff. Davis, the great Confederate Jupiter,
has appointed and commissioned me a Major General
of Confederate Volunteers, with my Idiotic Boy as
Chief of Staff, and has erected this part of the Confederacy into a military district, to be known as the
Department of Madisonville.

My first official act was to get blind drunk on Confederate whisky, after which I directed my Idiotic
Boy to issue my Proclamation, as follows:

Macpherson's Proclamation.

HEAD QRS. DEPAR'T MADISONVILLE,
Madisonville, La., May 10th, 1863.

General Order No. 1.

In accordance with the unparalleled glory and dignity which
now surround me, I hereby assume command of the army and

navy of the Department of Madisonville. I shall demand and enforce the fullest obedience to the Confederate Articles of War; and all male persons between the ages of ten and one hundred are hereby notified to report to me at once, armed and equipped for military service. Any citizen or resident of this Department, male or female, who shall hereafter pronounce the word "Yankee" without placing before it the Confederate adjective "damned," shall be hung without trial.

Soldiers and females of Madisonville! arise in your might and glory, and hurl the terrific thunderbolts of merciless vengeance against the United States! In me you have a leader worthy of your highest confidence and admiration, who will lead you to immediate victory and undying renown. With my own hand I will plant the victorious Stars and Bars on the Custom House of New Orleans, and on the St. Charles and City hotels; and sweeping with my legions like a besom of death-scattering destruction, I will not pause in my onward career of homicide and slaughter, until my unconquerable army shall enter the Arctic regions, and plant the almighty and overpowering flag of the Confederacy upon the North Pole, there to float as long as the all-nourishing earth shall revolve in the boundless and unfathomable realms of celestial space.

By order of MAJ. GEN. JAMES B. MACPHERSON.

THE IDIOTIC BOY, Chief of Staff.

The first extraordinary result of my promotion was an absorbing profanity, which compelled me to swear every time I opened my mouth; and I believe that my experience in this respect is similar to that of most military men. Whereas, but a few days before I stood in the pulpit and expounded the Confederate religion to a benighted world, and presented myself as a model of the Christian virtues and graces, and a strict temperance man, I found, the moment I put on a uniform, I was bound to swear like a Second Dragoon, and drink like the Tenth Infantry.

"Where is your army?" asked the Idiotic Boy.

"Damn the army!" I replied. "It is a peculiarity of Confederate warfare, that a Major General requires no army. Proclamations, sir, proclamations are the things with which to crush the Yankee foe. How did Beauregard raise the blockade of Charleston? With a Proclamation! How did Magruder do the same thing at Galveston? With a Proclamation! How did Governor Moore conscript the niggers in the Trans-Mississippi Department? With a Proclamation! Are they greater Generals than I? No, sir! You damned Idiot! talk to me about an army! I'll show you that I'm Major General and Commander of the Department. Pen, ink, paper, and gas are the only implements necessary to secure a Confederate victory at every step!" I then wrung the Idiot's nose and swore to be revenged.

Subsequently I determined to raise an army, and opened a Recruiting Office in Madisonville, and swore that I would fill the ranks at all hazards. I raised a Confederate flag two hundred feet long by Confederate measurement, which is four feet in Yankee mathematics, and sent a nigger through the streets pounding on a tin pan to drum up recruits. The first one that came in was seventy-four years of age, blind in one eye, walking on two crutches, and armed with a buzz-saw.

"Welcome!" I exclaimed, "young and ardent soldier of your country, to the headquarters of Confederate glory. You are the nucleus of the army of this department, and I will lead you to endless conquest!" He then whirled his buzz-saw and took his place in line-of-battle. I conscripted two niggers to hold him up on his crutches while he should fight.

Finding that this patriotic youth was the only person who would voluntarily enlist, or voluntarily obey my orders, I resolved to enforce my authority at the point of the sword, 'mid scenes of broil and battle. I therefore mounted the Confederate Mule, the same animal that carried me to New Orleans when I attended the great Charity Fair, and drawing my shining blade with a Confederate flourish, placed myself at the head of the column, determined to lead in person, according to Macpherson's Confederate Tactics, a profound work on military science, which I had compiled the night before. I marched off in the following order: 1st. The General Commanding, viz., myself. 2d. Music, viz., the nigger with a tin pan. 3d. The column in order of battle, consisting of the patriotic youth, supported on either flank by an African.

I determined to make my first demonstration on the abode of a Choctaw Indian, who had some time been seen about Madisonville dressed in the peculiar and fantastic style of his race. Halting in front, I gave the order to deploy column in the back yard, for the purpose of cutting off retreat, while I should attack in front, with the musician supporting me as a reserve. These dispositions having been made on scientific principles, I gave the Confederate snort, the great signal of attack. The Indian, started from his morning slumbers, without waiting to dress, jumped out of a side window and cut for the woods. "Sweet Choctaw!" I exclaimed, "for the moment thy speed gives thee success; but this is no fault of my tactics, and thou owest thy safety to the fact that I have not an adequate force to support my flanks. If thou thinkest

ine deficient in the art of war, try and make thine escape through the back yard, over my invincible column!" I then put spurs to my mule, and started in
pursuit. After a race of two miles, I overtook him
and held him, while, in obedience to my orders, the
column came up, and the Choctaw was conscripted,
and took his place in line of battle, a willing and obedient soldier of the Confederacy. "The Great Spirit,"
I said to him, "will not send any Choctaw to the
happy Hunting Grounds, unless he fights for the Confederacy." The column then marched back to Madisonville.

My Chief of Staff reported a case of gross and damnable insubordination, which I resolved to punish in
Confederate style, with the fullest extremity of military
vengeance. A young and able-bodied man, only sixty
years of age, living in the suburbs of the city of Madisonville, had disregarded the order to enlist, and had
concealed himself in the woods, armed with a shot-gun,
determined to die rather than take up arms against the
United States. I immediately ordered my forces,
white and Choctaw, to advance, and halted at the residence of the accursed Yankee. Dismounting, I entered the house, where I found a woman and five children. "Where," I demanded in tones of thunder,
flourishing my sword, and stamping my foot, "where,
woman, is thy Yankee husband!"

"Oh, sir!" said she, falling at my feet, and looking
imploringly in my face, "for the love of Heaven, spare
him! He is old and feeble, and we shall starve without him. We are poor and hungry, and he is our only
hope. Look upon my children, and pity us."

"What are children to me, or I to children?" I asked. "I am a Confederate General, sworn to win innumerable battles with this shining sword, and to exterminate the whole vile race of detested Yankees. Your husband shall die! He is a Yankee!"

"He is not a Yankee," said the woman; "he was born and raised in Louisiana."

"What do I care where he was born?" I answered. "Every man who does not fall down and worship Jeff. Davis and the Southern Confederacy, and is not willing to leave wife and children behind him to starve to death, for the sake of Southern independence, the same is a Yankee, and shall suffer death?" I then ordered the Choctaw Division to advance, with two bloodhounds thrown out in front, as skirmishers and detectives, and gave orders to bring the villain, alive if possible, but dead, if necessary. The Division gave the Choctaw warwhoop and advanced at the double-quick, and the bloodhounds soon got on the scent. In a few hours the accursed villain was brought to my headquarters, bleeding from wounds inflicted by my skirmishers.

"I am old and feeble," he began to say, "and wholly unable to bear arms."

"Silence!" I exclaimed. "Perhaps your benighted and besotted mind does not understand the great fundamental principles of Confederate Justice, so beautifully illustrated in the official career of General Hindman, who reprieved two men after they had been shot. It is a peculiarity in our system of jurisprudence, that we understand a case without asking any questions, and convict and punish a man without investigating

his case. I have Confederate brains in my head, and
it is as clear to me as the light which beams from the
all-beholding sun, that you are a Yankee Abolitionist.
You will, therefore, prepare for instant death."

A gallows was erected in front of his house, and he
was hung by the Choctaw Division, under my order.
As an act of mercy, I permitted his wife and children
to witness the execution.

Thus, in a single day, did I raise and equip a Confederate army, discipline them, put them on a war
footing, and win two battles. I retired for the night,
thankful for the success of my patriotic efforts, and
panting for glory upon the field of carnage.

Yours undeviatingly,
JAMES B. MACPHERSON.

CHAPTER XV.

MACPHERSON ENCOUNTERS AND SHOOTS A MIDNIGHT ASSAS-
SIN.—HE CONSCRIPTS NEGROES, AND ADDRESSES THEM IN
A MANNER CALCULATED TO AROUSE THEIR ZEAL IN THE CON-
FEDERATE CAUSE.—HE APPOINTS HIS STAFF, ETC., ETC.

NOTE.—In the following letter the author attempted to exhibit the
Southern method of treating negroes, and the inducements which the
Richmond Government might offer them to serve in their cause.——
"The Inconsolable Thug," who receives a staff appointment, is a gentleman whose history has been omitted in this volume. He had a physical fight with Macpherson, in which the Confederate Philosopher
was so badly worsted that he had to wear his head bandaged with
"a material poultice" for some weeks.

MADISONVILLE, LA.,
May 23, 1863.

SIR:—Arousing from a dream, I looked up and saw
a Midnight Assassin stealing into my room with fierce
looks, and with a dagger in his hand, which he pur-
posed to plunge into my vitals. This sight it was that
harrowed up my soul, froze my young blood, made my
two eyes, like stars, start from their spheres, my knot-
ted and combined locks to part, and each particular
hair to stand on end like quills upon the fretful porcu-
pine! "Is this a dagger which I see before me?" I
exclaimed: "or art thou but a dagger of the mind; a
false creation, proceeding from the rum-oppressed
brain? Avaunt! and quit my sight! Let the earth
hide thee!"

But the earth declined to do it, and the stealthy
Midnight Assassin, with murder in his heart and the

instrument of death in his hand, stood over me, ready
to perpetrate his crime of blood. . "Such," I thought,
"is the unhappy lot of greatness; to be exposed to the
shafts of malignant envy, to be watched, hunted, followed, assassinated! Oh that I were but an ordinary
man! Oh that nature had withholden from me the
prolific gifts of Genius, and the masterly qualities of a
military commander! Then I might have lived in
quiet seclusion and peace; but now I must die the victim of envied greatness!" It then occurred to me
that as a great Confederate General, it might be proper
to show fight, and die in heroic combat, falling with
my face to the foe. "What man dares, I dare!" I
exclaimed. "Approach thou like the rugged Russian
Bear, the armed Rhinoceros, or the Hyrean Tiger,
and my firm nerves shall never tremble!" As I said
this, the cold perspiration stood upon my forehead. I
then drew my Jeff. Davis revolver from under my
head, and shot the villain dead on the spot!

The moment I had committed this deed of homicide,
my conscience reproved me, and trembling with fear,
I wrapped my head up tight in the Confederate Blanket which always covers my martial couch. "I am,"
I said, "a foul and unnatural murderer; and if justice
dwells in Madisonville, I shall be hung by the neck
until I am dead!"

Aurora at last mounted her golden chariot, and the
light of morning shed its celestial lustre over the man-
inhabiting earth. But I, overcome by a consciousness
of guilty homicide, dared not look up for two hours.
Then I was moved by a conviction of duty, and wishing to drill my army in Confederate tactics, I resolved

to leap boldly from my couch, gaze indifferently upon
the mangled remains of my victim, and deny all knowledge of the transaction. Therefore, hurling the per-
spiration-besmeared blanket from my august person, I
leaped from the bed and opened my eyes, to fix them
on the dead corse of my red-handed homicide. But I
discovered that nobody was hurt. There was, however, a distinct bullet-hole in my Gray Confederate
breeches, that were hanging on a chair at the foot of
the bed; and these I had mistaken and shot for a Midnight Assassin.

The Madisonville Congo Guards.

Therefore, I determined to conscript all niggers
between the ages of nine and one hundred, within five
miles of Madisonville, and issued orders to that effect.
But the vile darkies did not heed my commands, and
I therefore deployed the buzz-saw Division as skirmishers, with orders to fetch in every nigger that
could be found. Ten of them were captured and
brought to my headquarters; whereupon I proceeded
to address them in a very able and patriotic manner,
both upon the destiny of articulate-speaking men, and
the duty of Confederate soldiers in the field, with the
hope of instilling into their besotted intellects some
gleamings of the lofty and humane philosophy of the
Confederacy.

"You damned niggers!" I said; "you are about to
be enrolled as Confederate soldiers, under the laws of
Louisiana, and in accordance with the proclamation of
Governor Moore. This is the highest honor that could

be bestowed even upon a white man, and for you to receive it is a blessing so vast and incomprehensible that none but a Mammoth Brain can understand the full and imperishable felicity that has descended into your black souls. But you will please understand that this is not a compliment to you personally, but to the Confederacy which you represent; and you will also comprehend distinctly that you are not human beings at all, and that the design of the Infinite was that you should be slaves and wild beasts forever. The Confederacy is based upon this divine law of nature, which made the Confederacy to boss and abuse niggers and keep them on a perfect equality with Confederate mules. You are the connecting link between man and the monkey, and differ from the Orang-Outang only in the gift of speech. This was given you by the Almighty, in order that you might better serve your masters; for everybody must admit that a dumb nigger will not bring as high a price in the market as those that can utter speech. Vice President Stephens has nobly said that niggers are the corner-stone of the Confederacy, and this I wish to impress upon your debased and idiotic minds. Your heels are long and your shins tender, and that proves the truth of Judge Taney's declaration, that you haven't any rights that white men ought to respect. The Lord cursed Ham, and the ham was smoked. Therefore you are black, damn you! and must be enslaved by the Confederates for evermore. I can prove it by the Confederate Bible; for the theology of the Confederacy, as I showed in my celebrated sermon from the words, 'Blow ye,' permits true believers to strike out any passage of Scripture they don't like, and to put in any thing they'd like to have there.

"Therefore it is that the Confederate Theology is superior to every other. You can prove any thing you want to by it, or you can confound every theory ever started or adopted by mortal man. The Confederate Bible is on a par with the Confederate Arithmetic, and I am the author of both. Therefore, let no nigger dispute my words, for I can prove every thing I say. You are niggers, and niggers are not men, and it is now your glorious privilege to fight for these divine principles of the Southern Confederacy—principles founded upon the great and everlasting law of Confederate veracity."

The effect of this splendid oration upon those to whom it was addressed, was, indeed, like magic. The bold declarations of truth smote upon their heathenish and bestial intellects, and inspired them with overpowering and matchless zeal for Southern Independence. They gave five hundred cheers for the Confederacy, and six hundred for me, and threw their hats a thousand feet in the air by Confederate measurement, while the biggest nigger, grinning from ear to ear, struck up the Old John Brown song, the whole Congo Division joining in the chorus: "Glory, glory, hallelujah!" Immediately the spirit of prophecy and of poesy descended upon me, and I composed a Confederate war-song, to be sung on all occasions, as follows:

6*

SONG OF THE CONGO GUARDS.

By James B. Macpherson, Author of the Confederate Arithmetic and the Hymn of Salvation.

1.

Oh the niggers they are monkeys and were born for slavery,
The niggers they are monkeys and were born for slavery,
Tho niggers they are monkeys and were born for slavery,
　　As we go fighting along.
　　　Glory, glory, hallelujah!
　　　Glory, glory, hallelujah!
　　　Glory, glory, hallelujah!
　　As we go fighting along.

2.

Oh the abolition Yankees they are a set of thieves,
The abolition Yankees, &c., &c.

I should have proceeded further with this beautiful production, but I have adopted the rule that I will never write a poem of more than two stanzas. I then proceeded to arm the Congo Division with sheep-shears, and issued the following General Order:

　　　　HEADQUARTERS,
　　DEPARTMENT OF MADISONVILLE,
　　　　Madisonville, La., May 20th, 1868.

General Order No. 2.

The General Commanding hereby gives notice that the following high-toned gentleman and officers will constitute his staff, and will be obeyed and respected accordingly until further orders:

THE IDIOTIC BOY, Chief of Staff.

THE HONEST JEW, Chief Quartermaster.

THE UNHAPPY CUSS, Chief Commissary.

THE SOLITARY HORSEMAN, Chief of Cavalry.

THE NOBLE WOMAN, Superintendent of the Great Confederate Clothing Emporium in New Orleans.

THE INCONSOLABLE THING, Chief of Artillery.

THE WEEPING ORPHAN, Judge Advocate.

THE SOUTHERN SOURCE, Chief of Signal Corps.

The officers above named will report immediately at the Great Confederate Clothing Emporium, in Canal street, and the ladies of New Orleans are hereby directed to furnish a uniform for each, out of the great Charity Fund.

By order of MAJOR GENERAL JAMES D. MACPHERSON.

THE IDIOTIC BOY, Chief of Staff.

It will be seen that in the above order I have followed the Confederate law of promotion, and given a posish to each of my friends. I shall make each of my nine sons a Brigadier General as soon as I can recruit nine men.

Yours, boldly,

JAMES B. MACPHERSON.

. ˙

CHAPTER XVI.

THE REGISTERED ENEMIES OF THE UNITED STATES LEAVE
THE DEPARTMENT OF THE GULF.—GENERAL MACPHERSON
SUPERINTENDS THEIR DEPARTURE.—HE "GOBBLES" THEM AS
SOON AS THEY ARRIVE IN HIS DOMINIONS.—HE UNEXPECT-
EDLY MEETS THE HONEST JEW, ETC., ETC.

NOTE.—On the 30th of April, 1863, an order was published by Major
General Banks, requiring all registered enemies of the United States
to leave the Department of the Gulf, on or before the fifteenth day
of the next month. As no one could sail for any port in the United
States or a foreign country without taking the oath of allegiance to the
United States, the registered enemies were compelled to go over to the
"Confederacy," for which they had professed such a profound rever-
ence and love. So long as they were forbidden to go, they were loud
in their complaints that the cruel and despotic government should
prevent them from joining their friends; but when they were ordered to go, all their zeal disappeared, and they were equally loud in
their complaints that the cruel and despotic government should compel them to go. When the time of their departure actually arrived,
they presented a melancholy spectacle; a more dejected set of wretches
was never seen. To add to their grief, as soon as they arrived in
Mobile, the able-bodied men were forced to join the rebel army. The
order sending them out of the Department was received with great
exultation by the Union citizens of New Orleans; for some of these
registered enemies had become very insolent, under the lenity that
permitted them to remain in the city. Many of them had registered
their names as enemies of the United States, in order to make themselves popular with the secessionists, and without any expectation
that they would ever be compelled to leave the Department. And
when they found that the fact of being registered enemies in-
volved the necessity of going away, and, as was the case with many,
of leaving home, family, and kindred behind them, perhaps forever,
the romance all melted into thin air, and they discovered that a sentimental attachment for the land of Jeff. Davis, which could be cher-
ished in security at a distance, was quite a different matter when it
exiled them from the comforts and pleasures of civilised life.

MADISONVILLE, LA.,
May 30th, 1863.

Sir :—A Macedonian cry came to me as in my dilapidated hospitable abode I meditated schemes of bloodshed and revenge. It came from New Orleans, from a Registered Enemy, and said : " What shall I do? Come over and help me!"

Arriving in New Orleans, I immediately called upon the Macedonian, and with him forthwith went down to Lakeport to witness the departure of the first regular load of Registered Enemies. " Now," I said, " there will be a grand secession demonstration, exceeding that on the levee, when the women turned out *en masse* to kiss the departing Confederate prisoners. I will summon the people to arms, raise a revolt, capture New Orleans, and add it to the Department of Madisonville!"

But when I arrived at the point of embarkation my soul and face became swollen with Confederate indignation. For instead of a grand secesh demonstration I only found a small crowd of weeping women and wailing children, who said they wished their husbands and fathers had taken the oath of allegiance to the United States, instead of running off to the Confederacy and leaving them to starve alone.

" Stop such treasonable talk as that!" I shouted in tones of Confederate thunder. " Every person who utters a sentiment favorable to the Union, will have his name written down, and he shall be hung when the Confederates come here!"

" What has the United States done so bad?" asked a woman who was weeping in a base and cowardly manner at the departure of her husband. " Did we not live together in peace and plenty before the South seceded? What wickedness did the United States commit?"

"It robbed us of eternal rights," I answered.

"Is it not the eternal right of a wife to be protected by her husband, and to have her children fed and cared for by their father?" asked she, in a violent flood of tears.

"Base, cowardly woman!" I exclaimed; "the great light of Confederate Science has never pierced your weak and debased intellect. Women and children, food and raiment, are nothing beside Southern Independence. Were it not for the rebellion, would I ever have been a Major General? No! Would Jeff. Davis have been a President? No! Would My Idiotic Boy have been Chief of Staff, or the Honest Jew a Quartermaster? No! Such, madame, are the happy fruits of rebellion. What to me are weeping women and starving children?—what desolate firesides and blasted fields? —what trenches of buried soldiers and plantations gone to waste? Nothing! These are the price of Confederate shoulder-straps and civic crowns. What though they are stained in innocent blood and bathed in woman's tears? They glitter all the same, and glory still summons the Confederate Warrior to the field! Starve, for ought I care! The more that starve, the less there will be to feed on the next crop!"

"You are an unfeeling brute!" sobbed the woman.

"Madame," I replied, drawing myself up to my full height, and smiting my breast with great dignity; "madame, if my position does not protect me from insult, my sex at least should be respected!"

I then turned away with an air of justly offended pride, and turned my eyes upon the black ship, about to depart for the lovely shores of my native land. I expected to see countenances gleaming with joy and patriotic pride. "These true and devoted friends of the Confederacy," I said, "have filled the earth with their moans, to be allowed to come to us, when they knew they couldn't; and now that they are at last allowed to come to our sweet land of cotton and independence, their faces will glow with unspeakable delight!" Imagine my burning wrath, when instead of this, I saw a pack of the most dejected devils that my eyes ever rested upon. One was looking at his wife and children with streaming eyes, and asking in a low moan if it was too late to take the Oath of Allegiance.

"Too late!" replied a Yankee Demon. Then the Registered Enemy smote his forehead with his hand, and said he had made a damned fool of himself, to which the Yankee Demon nodded assent.

"Beloved Confederates!" I said, addressing them from the shore; "as the Children of Israel, represented in Madisonville by the Honest Jew, wandered for forty years in the Wilderness, but at last found the happy land of Canaan, so have you, while twelve times the Moon hath filled her horn, borne with meek patience the unsufferable and loathsome bondage of the United States, sighing for the happiness of the Confederacy. But now the long night of your vassalage has been dispelled by the brilliant splendor of the rising Confederate Sun, and you are about to plant your weary feet in Madisonville, a land that flows with milk and honey, where the butchery of the Yankee Demons cannot disturb the quiet security of your throats, and where the Stars and Bars will stand between you and all harm."

Even this eloquence did not arouse their stupid souls, and I turned away in disgust, reluctantly concluding that the Registered Enemies were a lot of blockheads.

I immediately started for Madisonville on my Confederate Mule, in order to get there before the Registered Enemies reported at my headquarters.

Macpherson meets the Honest Jew.

As I was going hurriedly home, I saw a man in the woods tucking rolls of paper into the trunk of a hollow tree. Approaching him stealthily, I was astonished to recognize in him my integrity-loving friend and Confederate co-laborer, the Honest Jew. Wishing to give him a pleasant surprise, I caught him violently by the collar and planted my right foot stoutly against his shins, before he was aware of my presence.

He jumped eight feet in the air, and struck the ground, looking pale as a corpse, exclaiming with ferocious earnestness:

"I no steal 'em! I pe berfectly innocent!—berfectly innocent!"

"My innocent and outraged friend!" I replied, "of course you are innocent. Who accused you of stealing?"

"Gott im Himmel!" shouted the Honest Jew; "I taut you pe vun tam tief and robber. I now know you pe mine tear Sheneral." We then clasped each other in a tender, loving embrace, until our bosoms were bathed in tears of mutual love.

"A pleasant surprise, my dear," I said.

"Oh, yah, vun sehr tam bleasant surbrise," he answered.

"What have you here?" I asked, approaching the tree.

"Noting, noting at all," he answered.

"Then there can be no harm if I look at nothing," I answered, and then proceeded to examine the tree, when I discovered several very large rolls of Confederate treasury notes. "Sweet disciple of Moses," I said, "whence and for whom this vast treasure?"

"Mine!" he cried, while a look of agony passed over his features.

"Sir!" I said, "you are a swindler and thief! I am your superior officer, and I swear that unless you divide with me justly and fairly, I will hang you, and expose to the world your infamous crimes!"

The Honest Jew then swore he always intended to divide with me, and that he hid the bills only as a means of security. I then asked him how he had managed to accumulate such vast wealth.

"I sells the glothing and horses," he replied. I then learned that, after conscripting an army, the Honest Jew had drawn clothing and horses from the Government, and that he had sold the clothing to the soldiers and the horses to the highest bidder, and that the money in the tree was the fruit of this scheme, alike creditable to his head and heart.

"Nothing," I remarked, "but an equal distribution of the proceeds, could have reconciled me to this admirable trick. Come once more to my bosom!"

"I make you very rich in five tays," said the Honest Jew.

" How," I asked.

" You vait for the Registered Enemies," he answered.

Arriving at Headquarters, I found that great numbers of Registered Enemies had arrived and were arriving from New Orleans, and thereupon I immediately issued an order on the subject, as follows:

HEADQUARTERS,
DEPARTMENT OF MADISONVILLE,
Madisonville, La., May 28th, 1863.

General Order No. 3.

Whereas, it has come to the knowledge of the Major-General commanding this Department, that certain and numerous persons, pretending to be Registered Enemies of the United States have arrived within the limits of his command from New Orleans, it is therefore ordered: That all the Registered Male Enemies of the United States coming to these shores, not over one hundred years of age, shall be immediately conscripted and enrolled as a part of the military force of this Department; *unless* they shall pay over to the Chief Quartermaster the sum of one thousand dollars, in which case they shall be exempt from the draft.

By order of MAJOR GENERAL JAMES B. MACPHERSON.

THE IDIOTIC BOY, Chief of Staff.

The first Registered Enemy who reported himself at Headquarters was the Macedonian, who came with a smiling face, and, slapping me on the shoulder, said: " Our relations have been so pleasant heretofore, that I shall find in your sweet society full compensation for the sacrifice I make in leaving my native land." But I put on a look of offended dignity, and inquired who it was that presumed to make himself so familiar! I then handed him a copy of the above order, and he turned pale as a ghost when he read it. However, he paid one thousand dollars to the Honest Jew. In all five hundred men paid their thousand dollars, which made the handsome sum of five hundred thousand dollars to be equally divided between the Honest Jew and myself. I then issued the following:

HEADQUARTERS,
DEPARTMENT OF MADISONVILLE,
Madisonville, La., May 29th, 1803.

General Order No. 4.

So much of General Order No. 3, as relates to the Exemption of Registered Enemies from the operation of the Conscript law on payment of one thousand dollars, is hereby rescinded; and all Registered Enemies, without exception, will immediately report armed and equipped for military service, the same as though the said sum had never been paid.

By order of MAJOR GENERAL JAMES B. MACPHERSON.
THE IDIOTIC BOY, Chief of Staff.

"By what code of justice is it," inquired the Macedonian, "that, after taking our money on promise of exemption, you compel us to enter the service?"

"By the code of Confederate justice," I replied: "the same principle that is in force in New Orleans, which compels negro property-holders to pay taxes for the support of schools, and then forbids them to send their children to school; and the same principle by which John C. Breckinridge, sitting in the Senate of the United States, and drawing his salary from the United States treasury, plotted and toiled for the downfall of the Union, and the up-building of the Southern Confederacy."

Settlement with the Honest Jew.

At midnight, in my guarded tent, I summoned the Honest Jew to my presence, and told him we had made a million dollars, and it was time to divide. I therefore ordered him to settle immediately, and to pay over to me one-half the profits, in accordance with the bargain fairly agreed to by both parties.

"Show me your receipts," said the Jew; "I can bay no monish mitout receipts to show I owe it!"

"Loathsome and disgusting reptile!" I exclaimed, "is it thus you trifle with pecuniary rights and eternal justice? Is it thus you seek to subvert the principles of Confederate veracity, and uproot the very foundations of society? Can you expect to rob the Confederacy and its loyal subjects with impunity, and not divide the profits with your Commanding General! I will show you that it cannot be done. For half thy wealth, it is Macpherson's; the other half comes to the general State which I represent, and so I'll take the whole."

"Nay, take my life and all, pardon not that;" replied the Honest Jew, "you take my house when you do take the prop that doth sustain my house; you take my life when you do take the means whereby I live."

"Bring hither the cash and abjure thy vile faith, and thou shalt live and have half," I said.

"Yah," replied the Honest Jew, "I do that mit time. I goes now and pring you the monish."

He then started off to bring to my tent the treasure; and I lay congratulating myself that I had made half a million dollars, and converted a Jew to the true faith. But hour after hour passed, and the Honest Jew did not return. Two o'clock, three o'clock, four o'clock, daylight, and no welcome Mosaic footstep came to cheer me in my waiting loneliness.

"Oh Honest Jew!" I cried in my distress, "what evil hath befallen thee? Oh whither hast thou wandered? Did thy pious youthful feet go astray in the woods?" I then hastened to the hollow tree, hoping at least to find the treasure, even if I could not once more clasp the Honest Jew to my bosom in a loving embrace. But imagine my grief, terror, rage, when I discovered that the vile villain had gobbled up all the money and skedaddled to distant and unknown places, leaving me once more to groan and moan in honest poverty, the victim of loathsome and disgusting rascality.

Yours eternally,

JAMES B. MACPHERSON.

CHAPTER XVII.

AN ACCOUNT OF THE DEATH OF JAMES B. MACPHERSON,
THE GREAT CONFEDERATE PHILOSOPHER, WARRIOR, AUTHOR,
AND SOUTHERN BLOWER.

NOTE.—The author determined to discontinue Macpherson's Letters, and knew of no better way than to kill him off. Accordingly the following obituary notice was prepared and published in THE ERA of June 7th.

HUNG be the heavens with black!—yield day to night! Comets, importing change of times and States, brandish your crystal tresses in the sky, and with them scourge the bad revolting stars, that have consented to Macpherson's death!

It becomes our painful duty to announce to the world the death of JAMES B. MACPHERSON, of Madisonville, Louisiana, Major General of Confederate Volunteers, invincible warrior and pugilist, Plato of the Confederacy, Archimedes of the New Nation, Author of the celebrated Confederate Arithmetic, Traveller through the Louisiana Lowlands Low, Father of twelve sons, Clergyman, and Southern Blower—the scintillations of whose Ponderous Intellect have so long illuminated the columns of THE ERA. The Mammoth Brain of our revered correspondent no longer works; the Herculean Arm is no longer bared in the cause of the Confederacy he so faithfully and zealously represented; the tongue of persuasive eloquence has been silenced in the embrace of all-devouring Death! He expired at his dilapidated hospitable abode, in Madisonville, at the solemn hour of midnight, last Monday, being the six hundred and sixtieth Olympiad and the third year thereof, and the year 3 of the Southern Confederacy.

The cause of his death is melancholy beyond description. He did not fall in battle, as was his ardent desire, at the head of his invincible legions, dealing death and destruction among vile Yankee foes ; but he fell a victim to his own hands. In a word, he committed suicide. Calling his Idiotic Boy to his side, he exclaimed :

"Oh that this too too solid flesh would melt, thaw, and resolve itself into a dew ! or that the Everlasting had not fixed his canon 'gainst self-slaughter ! Now indeed I fear the avenging wrath of the offended gods of Olympus. But if I would reach the Elysian Fields, where dwells the soul of the great Achilles, I must die at once, like Socrates, the Philosopher, by drinking poisonous hemlock !"

Having announced his determination, his family and his staff in vain gathered around him with tears, striving to win him from his fatal purpose. They pointed out to him the deadly stroke the Confederacy would suffer; the pallor with which Philosophy and Religion would hear of his death ; the inconsolable tears of his wife and staff; the exultation of the Yankee Demon, and the honest grief of THE ERA. But all in vain. "I love the Confederacy with intense and passionate love," he answered, "but the will of the gods and the Voice of Oracular Fate must be obeyed !" He then ordered the hemlock to be brought to him in a five-gallon demijohn, and calmly entered upon the

business of preparation for his journey across the Styx,
—or to quote from his own beautiful words, for " the
coming of that solemn hour, when neither worldly
pomp, nor martial renown, nor yet the brave love of
the Confederacy which pervades every impulse of my
soul, and every throb of my heart, can stay my footsteps in the last pilgrimage to the realms of Pluto."

Macpherson's Will.

He then took four drinks of the hemlock, and proceeded to make his will, with all the calmness and dignity of Confederate greatness.

"To my faithful and beloved wife," he said, "I give
and bequeath my dilapidated hospitable abode, and
all it contains; to my Idiotic Boy, the mantle of Philosophy and the management of Confederate Policy; to
my staff, I give my sword and uniform, and it is my
wish that after my death they shall contend for it in
single combat, as Ulysses and Telamonian Ajax contended for the armor of divine Achilles; and to the
combatants for the splendid prize, I say in the words
of man-smiting Heenan, *may the best man win!*

"To the Noble Woman and the ladies of New
Orleans, I leave the task of fanning and keeping alive
the fires of treason in the Yankee-oppressed Crescent
City."

Having made the above disposition of his worldly
affairs, he took four drinks of the hemlock, and remarked that the working of the Mammoth Brain would
cease the moment the working of the fatal hemlock
began.

"To the Unhappy Cuss," he said, "I leave the arrangements for the funeral. I wish to be buried with military honors worthy of my rank and name. I wish to have my funeral modelled on that of Alexander the Great, a warrior whose fame was only surpassed by my own. In the third Section of the sixteenth Book of Rollin's History, you will find an account of the ceremonies performed at the interment of the Conqueror of the World; and I wish those performances to be carried out to the letter, over my own remains."

At this stage of the solemn scene, there was a loud wail heard in the door, and looking around there was seen the Honest Jew, pale and haggard, and bathed with tears. He fell upon the floor, rolled over, threw himself upon the neck of the expiring Philosopher, tore his hair, and asked to be forgiven.

"To err is human—to forgive divine!" answered the dying General. "Your arrival is most opportune, for the treasury is empty and the preparations for my funeral will involve an immense outlay. Promise to defray these expenses, and I will forgive you all."

"I promise," said the Honest Jew; and then the two great men, happily reconciled, embraced with touching affection.

"It has been the great purpose of my life," said the expiring Warrior, "to re-establish in all its glory the worship of the Olympian gods; for the pagan religion alone, with such additions as I have made, is fitted to the demands of the Confederacy. But I am cut off by Fate in the midst of my labors, and I desire to be buried after the manner of the Greeks and Romans."

Midnight at last cast the shadow of deepest gloom

over the face of universal nature. The great Macpherson had now nearly emptied the demijohn, and all felt conscious that the fatal hemlock must soon do its horrible work. Suddenly he gave a wild groan, and, rising in his couch, smote his breast and spake his last words, as follows:

Last Words of Macpherson.

"The long day has passed," he exclaimed; "the long night is come! O Jupiter! thou great father of gods and men, the most high and powerful among the immortals, whom all others obey! avenge the wrongs of the Confederacy, and smite the Yankees with the bolts of thy thunder! Farewell, brave Staff! Carry out the policy which I have inaugurated, imitate my valor, and always buy your hats of Stapleton, 95 Canal-street."

A cold sweat then stood upon his intellectual brow; the eyes became fixed, the lips ceased to move, and JAMES B. MACPHERSON, the great light of Confederate letters, the favorite of the ladies of New Orleans, ceased to breathe the vital air.

We have the authority of the Southern Source, a member of his staff, for saying that prodigies of nature attended the departure of the valorous chieftain to the realms of Pluto. He informs us that cloud-compelling Jove, at the moment of dissolution, hurled a living bolt of thunder from Mount Olympus, which smashed the five-gallon demijohn, that had held the impious poison, into a thousand atoms, and tore the musquito bar worse than was torn that one which Mac-

pherson described in the great Temple of Wisdom at
Brashear City.

Long and bitterly did his staff and his friends gaze
upon his serene countenance; not even the pallor of
death could erase the lineaments of thought or hide
the phrenological developments of the Mammoth
Brain. Then the Honest Jew brought in a coffin of
baked clay, and every thing was prepared for the im-
posing ceremonies of the interment, which were performed with great pomp, and were an exact copy of
those performed in honor of Alexander the Great, except that Macpherson's chariot was trimmed with brass
instead of gold. The following inscription, composed
by Macpherson himself, was placed over his Tomb, at
his own request:

JACOBUS B. MACPHERSON.

ILLUSTRISSIMUS,

SCRIPTOR, POETA, MATHEMATICUS, FŒDERATUS,
PRÆDICATOR, MILES EXERCITATUS. JOVI, FILIUS
TERTIUS, HERCULIS ET BACCHI FRATER, FŒDERIS
AUSTRALIS PLATO, ET PERIORINATOR CELEBERRI-
MUS.

IMMATURA MORTE ADRIEPIEDATUR OLYMPIADIS
SEXCENTESIMÆ ET SEXCENGESIMÆ ANNO TERTIO,
ET FŒDERIS AUSTRALIS ANNO TERTIO.

DEOS OLYMPIACOS ADORABAT, ET UT IN CAM-
PIS ELYSIIS MANES ACHILLIS CONJUNGERET, E
VITA CEDEBAT.

Our task is accomplished; our mournful duty is done.
If the Southern Confederacy has lost its brightest or-
nament, the Editor of The Era has lost his most high-

falutin contributor.   In conclusion, we have to ac-
knowledge our indebtedness to the Idiotic Boy, and
other members of General Macpherson's staff, for the
particulars of his death. The great Philosopher and
hero who has departed, has often reminded our readers
that man is mortal, and that earthly greatness soon
vanishes, like the dews in the sunshine of the unclouded
heaven. Let each take the lesson home, remembering
that even the Mammoth Brain of Macpherson had to
succumb to the power with which earth's greatest men
have contended in vain. There is no fountain of perpetual youth, even in the Southern Confederacy, nor
yet in Madisonville, a place which Macpherson assured
us flows with milk and honey !

CHAPTER XVIII.

The Resuscitation of Macpherson.—It is Discovered that he was not Dead, only Dead Drunk.—His Method of Paying Debts.—He makes the Acquaintance of the Reliable Gentleman, etc., etc.

Note.—During the siege of Port Hudson, New Orleans was daily filled with rumors of disasters to the army of General Banks, which were industriously circulated by the secessionists. Men apparently made it their principal business to lounge around the St. Charles Hotel, and to retail these unfounded reports. Every statement made by the "Reliable Gentleman" in his conversation with Macpherson, the author himself heard at different times in that building. The noise made by piling wood on the levee was, on one occasion, mistaken for the roar of artillery by some negroes; and from this incident arose a report of a disastrous repulse of our army.——Macpherson was resuscitated in obedience to what appeared to be a very general demand on the part of the readers of THE ERA.——The Registered Enemies who went from New Orleans to Mobile, carried most astounding news. On their statements one of the Mobile papers issued an extra announcing that New Orleans had been captured by the Confederates under Magruder, who immediately started for Forts Jackson and St. Philip with a force of fifteen thousand men.——It may be proper, in this connection, to state that during the siege of Port Hudson, a formidable force of Texans advanced into Western Louisiana, with the intention of taking the fort at Donaldsonville (a village about eighty miles above New Orleans), cutting off the supplies of General Banks, seizing all the vessels that could be found, crossing the river and making a descent upon New Orleans. This force was variously estimated at ten thousand to eighteen thousand men. The plans of the rebels were frustrated by two serious defeats—one at Lafourche Crossing, and the other at Donaldsonville. The defense of the fort at the latter place was one of the most brilliant of the war. The garrison consisted of about a hundred and fifty men, under command of Major Bullen, and many of these were convalescents. The attacking force, under General Greene, consisted of an entire brigade. The gunboat Princess Royal, under Commander Woolsey, checked the advance of the enemy. A desperate hand-to-hand fight occurred, the

enemy advancing to the parapet. A hundred and twenty rebel prisoners were actually captured by the garrison, inside the works.
About a hundred of the enemy's dead were buried by our soldiers;
and the rebel loss in killed, wounded, and prisoners was about four
times us large as the entire force defending the place. Our loss was
inconsiderable. The fight at Lafourche Crossing was also a brilliant
affair. There were, in fact, two engagements, in both of which the
enemy was repulsed with severe loss. Colonel Cahill and Colonel
Stickney gained great credit in the successful defense of the place.
General Emory was at that time in command of the defenses of New
Orleans, and no officer could have performed his duties more vigilant-
ly or faithfully. The capture of Brashear City, and the erection of
rebel batteries on the river, threatened to sever all communication with
General Banks's forces at Port Hudson, and New Orleans itself was
menaced. The secessionists were in constant expectation of the arrival of a rebel army, for many days; and the Union citizens, as well
as the officers in command, were not certain their expectation would
not be realized. General Shepley, Military Governor of the State, called
upon the people to rally for the defense of their homes, and formed a
brigade for sixty days' service. General Emory called for negro volunteers, and two regiments were promptly raised.——The author has
deemed it proper to make these explanations, in order to show the
reader what a fruitful field New Orleans presented, in those days, for
"Reliable Gentlemen" and "Intelligent Contrabands."

MADISONVILLE, LA,
June 27th, 1863.

Sir:—I died in the consoling faith that I was the
Biggest Liar in the Southern Confederacy; but after
the arrival of the Registered Enemies in Alabama, I
found they were going so far ahead of me in that line,
that I should have to rise from my grave and vindicate
my noble reputation by the invention of more sublime
falsehoods than ever before graced my able productions. In truth, the mendacious stories those unhappy
exiles spread in the streets of Mobile actually made my
bones rattle in their coffin; and I came forth like that
mythological giant whose name I have forgotten; but
who, smitten to the earth, always arose with renewed

strength; and I will now tell such astounding lies as shall cause the Yankees to howl and the Confederacy go mad in the ecstasies of bliss!

An account of my death and burial has been published, and a Latin inscription placed on my tomb, so ponderous and incomprehensible that all hope of resuscitation seemed to be at an end. It was given out that I had committed self-slaughter, by drinking poisonous hemlock from a five-gallon demijohn. But the truth is, I was not dead, but only dead drunk, and the hemlock was only ordinary Louisiana Rum.

Alexander the Great drank the health of his friend Proteas in the Cup of Hercules, a Dutch Lager Beer arrangement, that held six bottles. He pledged his friend the second time in this enormous bumper, and immediately fell flat and died. Socrates, the greatest philosopher of the Greeks, as I am of the Confederates, took one swig of hemlock, and expired. In order to show myself superior to both of these, I drank the five gallons of Louisiana Rum, convinced that it is more fatal than the liquid consumed by Alexander, or the hemlock imbibed by Socrates. But I played dead to see what the newspapers would say about me, and what action would be taken by the Confederate Government.

Much to my astonishment, the Yankee ERA was the only paper in New Orleans that paid any attention whatever to my death. The others had been profuse in their tears over Stonewall Jackson; they had made themselves and their readers perfectly miserable over every two-penny Confederate hero who got killed or drank himself to death; but when I, who had always

praised them—I, who had been the champion of their
creed, and lied on the same side—I, Macpherson, the
great and shining light of the Confederacy, the Invincible Warrior and the most magnificent Blower the
Confederate Sun ever shone upon in all his course—I
say, when I, greater and wiser than all, was supposed to
be dead and gone to my grave, they had not a tear to
shed for me; not a black column-rule with which to
express an emotion of grief; not even a line among the
editorial notices of auction sales and health-restoring
patent pills, to announce the destruction of my noble
mind, and the overthrow of the greatest Intellect that
the world has ever known. Then it was I found how
sharper than a serpent's tooth it is to have a cussed
fool for a friend.

Macpherson comes forth.

Wednesday evening, June 17th, in the third year of
Confederate Independence, was the anniversary of the
Yankee battle of Bunker Hill, where the ragged
American militia clinched boldly with the British
Regulars. The pale new moon presented the faintest
possible crescent outline of beautiful silver, sinking
into the boundless expanse of Western Louisiana, when
I arose in all the habiliments with which the Honest
Jew had clothed me, and proceeded to my D. H. A.
(said initials being a classical abbreviation for my
Dilapidated Hospitable Abode).

As I entered that renowned mansion, more famous
than the White House at Washington, or the Pewter
Mug of New York, the Idiotic Boy fell flat on the

floor, overcome with strange unearthly fear, and cried aloud : " Tell me why thy canonised bones, hearsed in death, have burst their cerements ; why the sepulchre wherein we saw thee quietly inurned, hath oped his ponderous and marble jaws to cast thee up again ! What may this mean, that thou, dread corse, again in complete steel, revisitest thus the glimpses of the moon, making night hideous ?"

" Dry up ! " I replied, at the same time hitting him in the chops, and loudly demanding a drink of gin.

Macpherson pays his Debts by a General Order.

I found a vast number of bills from all quarters, and claimants immediately besieged my dwelling, demanding instant payment.   In the first place, there was the Confederate tailor, with a bill of $18,000 for my outfit as a Major General, who said his family was starving, and nothing but prompt liquidation would save them and him from famine.

" Prompt liquidation is my rule," I replied, and immediately took four drinks.

Then came the butcher with a similar bill for six months' supply of sole-leather steak ; then the grocer, the shoemaker, and so on to the end of the chapter. " Something must be done for these mudsills of society," I said.   " It is one of the evils of our existence, that laboring men have to eat and wear clothes ; and were I to suggest improvements in the formation of the Universe, I would arrange it that the mudsills who wait upon the Southern aristocracy, should grow fat on air, and look with contempt on base pecuniary

7*

means. I must at once pay these debts; and the devil
of it is, there isn't a dime in the treasury!"

Then it was that light burst upon me from South
Carolina, the great fountain of Southern Independence.
Then it was that I remembered that on the 6th day of
June, 1861, Governor Pickens paid all the debts of the
South by a proclamation, declaring it to be treason for
a Southerner to pay up in cash. Therefore I deter-
mined to relieve my creditors, and pay all bills by a
General Order; and accordingly I issued the follow-
ing:

HEADQUARTERS, DEP'T OF MADISONVILLE,
Madisonville, La., June 18th, 1863.

General Order No. 0.

Having come to life after consuming five gallons of Louisiana
Rum, and having again assumed command of this Department, and
having been pained at the sufferings of my deserving creditors,
and annoyed by their impertinent supplications for payment, in
order to relieve them and me by an ingenious Confederate device,
it is hereby ordered and declared as follows:

1. It shall be regarded as treason for the Major General commanding this Department, or any of his staff, to pay any tailors'
bills, butchers' bills, grocers' bills, promissory notes, or debts of
any description whatever.

2. Any person presenting a bill to the Major General commanding this Department, or any member of his staff, or demanding
payment for articles supplied, shall be guilty of misprision of treason, and shall be punished with death by hanging, and his estate
and personal effects shall be confiscated to the personal use and
possession of the Major General commanding this Department.

By order of MAJOR GENERAL JAMES B. MACPHERSON.

THE IDIOTIC BOY, Chief of Staff.

The Reliable Gentleman.

The Unhappy Cuss and myself then started for New
Orleans, to get the latest intelligence. Arriving at the

St. Charles Hotel, we put up for the night, when a man came up, and pulling me to one side, asked what the news was from Madisonville. I replied that I had not the honor of his acquaintance, and that he would do better to mind his own business, and not exhibit any of his impertinence to a Major General of Confederate Volunteers.

Hereupon the fellow drew himself up with great dignity, until he looked quite tall, and said:

"R. G. S. C. H."

"I am familiar with every language," I replied, "known to articulate-speaking men, since the accident at the tower of Babel; I understand all science and philosophy: I am, in fact, an Encyclopædia of Useful Knowledge, revised and enlarged; but I cannot, with all my learning, master those mystic symbols."

"I am," said the offended fellow, "the Reliable Gentleman of the St. Charles Hotel!"

"Come to my arms, sweet one!" I cried, clasping him to my heaving bosom in a loving embrace. "I regret that the Southern Source is not here to make your acquaintance; for there is such a remarkable resemblance in your personal appearance, impudent manners, and unblushing mendacity, that you might be mistaken for twins, or for one and the same person."

The Reliable Gentleman bowed profoundly, and replied: "I am proud, General; you do me infinite honor. I am, so to speak, the Ears of the St. Charles; for I hear every thing."

"Judging from the enormous development of your acoustic organs," I replied, looking admiringly at his ears, "I am fully prepared to believe your statement."

Again the Reliable Gentleman bowed his pleasure.
" I am," he continued, " the Repository of all information; nothing occurs without my knowledge; I am,
sir, a Boiling Caldron, wherein are thrown all scraps
of information, to be cooked up into reliable intelligence; and as the witches of Macbeth threw poisoned
entrails, fillet of snake, tongue of dog, adder's fork, and
lizard's leg into their caldron, so does every Big Liar
hurl his reliable information to me. I button-hole
every man I see; I pump him until he tells all he
knows and all he don't know; and I spread the news
around town, adding such suggestions as will please the
person to whom I speak."

" Dear Caldron !" I replied, kissing him fondly,
" you are the man I have long desired to find. Come
now, sit down, and tell me all that has happened during
the last four or five weeks."

You should have seen the dignity and pride which
then sat enthroned upon the countenance of the Boiling Caldron and Repository, as he drew himself up,
apparently believing that he was an India Rubber
Man, and could stretch himself out as tall as Honest
Old Abe, if he but put himself to it. I own I never saw
Wisdom until I looked upon that majestic countenance.
Retiring to the front of the Rotunda, and placing our
feet higher than our heads, the Reliable Gentleman
proceeded to give me the following additional particulars :

" During the period you mention," he said, impressively, " the bloodiest battle ever fought on this Continent has taken place at Port Hudson. Shiloh, Fort
Donaldson, Malvern Hill, were as a drop compared

to the red ocean of blood which there flooded the land."

"Which whipped?" I inquired.

"The advantage was decidedly with our arms," he replied; "but the victory was on the side of the enemy."

The Reliable Gentleman was about to proceed with his narrative, when he suddenly espied an Intelligent Contraband on the opposite side of the street. Quicker than Olympian lightning he darted off, seized him by the button-hole, and showered upon him a series of questions in such rapid succession, that the Intelligent Contraband was almost paralysed.

"Dey's at it, massa!" said I. C.

"At what?" inquired R. C.

"Fightin' up dar!" was the reply; "I'se hearn 'em!"

Immediately the Reliable Gentleman rushed frantically through the streets, grabbing every man he met, and telling him that a bloody battle was in progress up the river; that he had just seen a highly respectable gentleman direct from the battle-field, and that the slaughter was dreadful. Immediately the street corners were crowded by an excited populace, eagerly devouring the news, and repeating it with wild exaggerations. Soon the Intelligent Contraband approached me, and said: "Dar's a mistake, massa. Dat ar fightin' noise was dem niggers on the levee, pilin' up wood!"

The Reliable Gentleman then returned, and resumed the history of events. "A negro regiment went in a thousand strong," he said, "and seven hundred of them fell dead on the first fire. The slaughter was terrible. One was caught and hung, and three escaped lame for

life. Thirty-five Federal Generals were killed on the spot.
The slaughter was awful. Federal loss in two hours,
seventeen thousand five hundred and two. Meantime,
General Johnston concentrated a force of ninety-seven
thousand in General Banks's rear, ready and willing to
tear him in pieces. General Banks and staff were captured, and Colonel Grierson, with his whole command.
The slaughter was frightful. General Breckinridge next
made his appearance in General Banks's rear, with an immense force, and just before he arrived at Jackson, sent a
nigger to General Banks, to let him know that he was in
his rear. On the 3d of June, General Banks raised the
siege, and, with his whole command, retreated to Baton
Rouge, which place was subsequently captured by the
enemy. The slaughter was appalling. Kirby Smith
then crossed the river at Bayou Sara, moved towards
Port Hudson, and got into General Banks's rear, with
an immense force, sufficient to crush him, while Sibley,
just returned from a flying visit to Texas, hung upon his
flanks with a tremendous force. The slaughter was
unparalleled. General Taylor, about this time, got in
General Banks's rear. A portion of General Banks's
forces were then sent to Vicksburg to reinforce General
Grant. About this time a detachment of General
Grant's army was sent to the aid of General Banks,
from Vicksburg. The slaughter was tremendous!"

Here the Reliable Gentleman put on a look of such
awful wisdom and solemnity that I thought I should
die. If my Idiotic Boy knew twice as much as that
man, I'd make him Grand Blow-Master of the Confederacy. He then looked around with his fingers on
his lips, indicative of profound secrecy, and making sure

that no one could overhear him, made the following confidential communication: "Every human being in Western Louisiana, white and black, old and young, has been put to death! Every house, barn, shed, outhouse, tree, stump, shrub, cotton-bale, and combustible substance of every name and sex, was burned by the torch of the incendiary! The country is depopulated; the human race in that part is extinct, and the inhabitants are suffering all the torments of famine!"

Having delivered this crushing and reliable announcement, he started for the Bar-Room in great haste, and I left instantly for Madisonville, satisfied that the services of the Great Confederate Blower were not required in New Orleans.

Yours, sufficiently,
JAMES B. MACPHERSON.

CHAPTER XIX.

MACPHERSON ENCOUNTERS THE CUSSED FOOL OF CARONDELET-
STREET.—BETTING ON VICKSBURG AND PORT HUDSON.—
FOURTH OF JULY CELEBRATION AT MADISONVILLE, ETC., ETC.

NOTE.—The Union citizens of New Orleans will not soon forget the
unbounded joy inspired by the news of the capture of Vicksburg and
Port Hudson. The rebels stoutly refused to believe that either place
had fallen, and pronounced both reports "Yankee lies." They talked
loudly, and offered to bet against odds; but it was found that when
brought to the test, they generally "backed out."

MADISONVILLE, LA.,
July 18th, 1863.

SIR:—As I was sitting in Jacobs's Picture Gallery,
undergoing Photography, I chanced to cast my eyes
upon the sidewalk, and there I saw a CUSSED FOOL,
whom I knew at once was a good Confederate. Therefore I rushed out, without waiting to bid my friend
good-day, or to pay my bill, and clasping him warmly
by the hand, asked him what he was driving at.

"Betting," he replied.

"What are you betting on?" I asked him.

"On Vicksburg," replied the Cussed Fool.

"What's the matter with Vicksburg?" I asked.

"Nothing," he answered; "and that's what's the
matter with me. Come to my place in Carondelet-
street, and I will show you something that will make
your Confederate eyes gleam with joy."

Walking to his place I was delighted to find that he
was none of your poor white trash, but an out-and-out

Southern aristocrat. We took four drinks of wine, and I told him it was very choice, but that for an honest, steady drink, Louisiana Rum could not be beaten.

"Now then," said he, "I am going to prove to you by the Confederate Arithmetic that Vicksburg is not taken, and that the dispatch published by the Yankee editor of THE ERA was a foul and infamous invention—a lie made out of whole cloth, for a bad purpose, which, it is supposed, was to affect the price of sugar and molasses, etc."

"Proceed," I said, "for I am author of the Arithmetic of which you speak."

"In the first place," said he, "Vicksburg is impregnable. It is a Gibraltar, as I can prove to you by all the Southern papers that have published any thing on the subject." He then took down a file of Southern papers and pointed out eight thousand places in which Vicksburg was called "Gibraltar," and declared to be "impregnable." "Now," he continued, "the combined forces of France and Spain were unable to reduce Gibraltar, and a place that is impregnable cannot be taken, according to my views. But when we come to analyse the question we find that the intrenchments of Vicksburg are equal to twenty thousand men by the usual estimate, and this multiplied by fifty, according to Confederate mathematics, would make the works equal to one million of men. One Confederate is equal to five Yankees, and this would bring it up to five millions of men. Then we will take the garrison, which amounts to forty thousand. This sum multiplied by fifty gives us a garrison of two millions, each of whom is equal to five Yankees, and so, in fact, the garrison is ten millions strong. The garrison and the intrenchments together

thus give us fifteen million brave Southern patriots, all
armed and ready to fight with desperate valor for Confederate independence.   That nearly equals the entire
population of the free States, and if they cannot hold
out against Grant's army, then I will sell out and go to
France."

" You satisfy me," I replied, " I am sure that Vicksburg is not taken !"

" I'll bet ten thousand dollars on it !" passionately
cried the Cussed Fool.   .

Just then a Yankee came up, and said : " I'll take
that bet :"

" What !" cried the Cussed Fool, in amazement.

" I'll take the bet," he repeated, and at the same time
put down ten one thousand dollar greenbacks.

A smile of wonder passed over the face of the Cussed
Fool, as he surveyed the Yankee from head to foot, as
though he had been a curiosity in Barnum's Museum.

Understanding his meaning, I proceeded to explain :
"You Damned Yankee," I said, "you do not understand the principles of well-regulated Southern families.
When a man says he will bet on the Confederacy or
that Vicksburg is not taken, do you suppose he means
it ?   Not a bit of it !   It is an ordinance with the great
doctrine of Blowing ; a doctrine which I preached in
the Temple of Confederate Holiness in Camp street,
and which is faithfully followed by every secessionist in
New Orleans."

" That's true," said the Cussed Fool of Carondelet-
street.   "I'll not bet a dime ; put up your money !
But I know a man who will bet ten thousand dollars to
one thousand that Vicksburg is not taken."

"Show him to me," said the Damned Yankee.

We then walked down to Hawkins's, and there we found him. His face was red and swollen with blowing, and immediately I recognized him as the Great Southern Snorter. He *knew* it was a lie—he had seen a paper of a later date, and Vicksburg held out and was impregnable. He was ready to bet ten to one, up to any amount, that the Yankee dispatch was a lie.

"Up to what amount, sir?" inquired the Yankee.

"Up to any amount you please!" cried he, at the same time sending out a peculiar blowing sound from his nostrils.

"Say ten thousand," replied the Yankee.

"Say any thing you please!" cried the Great Southern Snorter.

"I say, then," replied the Yankee, "that I'll bet you ten thousand dollars against five thousand that Vicksburg has been taken by General Grant!"

"You must excuse me," said the great Southern Snorter, "I just remember that I have an imperative engagement. I have no time to talk with you, and, besides, if I should bet, most likely I would get arrested." The great Southern Snorter then walked off with a sad look, and all the Yankees laughed.

Just then a fiendish newsboy came up, and thrusting papers in our faces, cried out: "Here's your Extra Era—*Fall of Port Hudson !*"

"Its another Yankee lie!" cried the Cussed Fool; "I'll bet ten thousand it is a lie! I can prove that Port Hudson is impregnable and the Gibraltar of the Lower Mississippi!" He then ran the sum over on the ends of his fingers, as a devout Catholic would count th

bends, and I was pleased to see that he had the whole
Confederate Arithmetic at his tongue's end. "Garrison,
10,000 by 50 is 500,000, by 5 is 2,500,000. Fortifica-
tions, ditto is ditto; total number of Confederates,
5,000,000! The whole Yankee army could not contend
with one-tenth part of that number, and I *know* that
Port Hudson is not taken!"

How the Rebellion saved Property.

We then walked off, arm-in-arm, the Cussed Fool in
a most thoughtful abstracted mood.

"Fool," I said, "you are one of the best Confederates I have seen, and I now wish to ask what you and
the rest of the Confederates got up this rebellion for?"

"To save our property," he replied.

Just then we observed a red auction flag in front of
a most beautiful residence, and halting at the door, we
discovered TYLER in all his glory, selling the furniture
and every thing else at auction. "This," said the
Cussed Fool, "is a sale by order of the Quartermaster;
the house and furniture were confiscated and sold by
the United States, because the former owner was in the
Confederate army. Now see his splendid furniture, his
mirrors framed with massive gold, his statuary of
Carrara marble, his pianos, his library, all and every
thing put up for sale by Yankees, and bid off by Yankee purchasers, and the fruits thereof going into the
treasury of the United States, a government that every
Confederate despises."

"Where are his niggers?" I asked.

"Niggers!" shouted the Cussed Fool, while a flash

ing glow of pain overspread his fine face; "echo answers, Where? They have skedaddled, and refuse to return. They have enlisted or found employment elsewhere, and the proprietor thereof may say, in the words of the poet: 'Never again shall I behold thee!'"

"And this is the way you saved his property by the rebellion!" I remarked.

"Macpherson," said the Cussed Fool, "if the Southern Confederacy should bust up, I'm going to France."

"Go it," I replied, and whistled the new Confederate air of "*Lee in Pennsylvania.*"

July 4th—*Magruder in New Orleans.*

On the 4th of July, the people of Madisonville assembled in a vast multitude around my residence, and demanded an oration. The Idiotic Boy read the Confederate Declaration of Independence, which, for want of a table, he rested upon the head of a nigger. I then mounted a soap-barrel, and proceeded to expatiate on the beauties of Southern Independence. "It is eighty-seven years ago to-day," I said, "that George Washington and John B. Floyd laid the foundations of the Southern Confederacy, by proclaiming to the nations of the civilised world the eternal and heaven-ordained doctrine of secession. But it took Jeff. Davis and the Miles Legion to complete the noble work; and it was not until the year 1861 that Truth, robed in light gray, and bearing a Palmetto tree in her hand, stepped forth from the shores of South Carolina, and clasping Jeff. Davis and A. H. Stephens in her arms,

carried them to Richmond, there to found a dynasty
more permanent than that of Denmark Vesey or Gov.
Dorr, of Rhode Island."

During the inspiring ceremonies of this great celebration, the Buzz Saw Division paraded under arms,
and the Honest Jew peddled jewelry among the crowd.
I then had the following General Order read aloud,
and the vast assembly dispersed to their respectable
abodes:

> HEADQUARTERS,
> DEPARTMENT OF MADISONVILL ,
> Madisonville, La., July 4th, 1863.

General Order No. 7.

1. The General Commanding felicitates the people of his Department on the recent brilliant Confederate Victories at Port
Hudson and Vicksburg, and also in Pennsylvania and Tennessee.
The splendid valor of our troops has demonstrated to the world
that an impregnable Gibraltar cannot be taken, and that an invincible warrior cannot whipped.

2. General Magruder, having captured the city of New Orleans
and Forts Jackson and St. Philip, will immediately report to me
for duty at these headquarters.

3. The city of New Orleans and vicinity are hereby annexed to
the Department of Madisonville.

By order of Major General JAMES B. MACPHERSON:

> THE IDIOTIC BOY, Chief of Staff.

The Philosophy of Honesty.

Before leaving the Cussed Fool, I asked him to de-
fine Honesty, and he replied that it consisted of forming an opinion and sticking to it through thick and
thin, in spite of facts or arguments. "The man," said
he, "who lives up to his faith at the greatest sacrifice
of comfort, money, and common sense, is the most
honest man. Tell me who you think he is."

I replied as follows: "I agree with your definition, and in my opinion Brigham Young is the most honest and self-sacrificing man on this Continent. He believes in Bigamy, and lives up to his creed by maintaining forty wives, thus depriving him of every earthly comfort to illustrate the great principle of his creed!"

Yours, heroically,
JAMES B. MACPHERSON.

CHAPTER XX.

THE PHANTOM CONFEDERATE; OR, THE GHOST OF MADISON-
VILLE.

(A True Story.)

MADISONVILLE, LA.,
August 1, 1863.

SIR:—It was in the full of the Moon, in the month called Julius by the Romans, and anno tertio de la Southern Confederacy, at the very witching hour of night, when churchyards yawn, and hell itself breathes forth contagion to the world, that I might have been seen seated on a cypress stump, in the midst of a blasted heath, near the classical city of Madisonville, C. S. A., with a roll of plug tobacco in my hand, (a present from Gov. Lubbock, of Texas), and a Confederate canteen of Louisiana Rum by my side. Thus sitting did I meditate upon that beautiful scene described by Virgil, in which Æneas, with his Trojan followers, as ragged and dirty as a Confederate army, was visited by Venus, his good-looking mother, who came in the form of a huntress, with a commodious bow hanging from her white shoulders. *O Dea certe!* cried the pious Æneas; which, being translated into the Confederate tongue, means: *O goddess for certain!* "Why," thought I, "if goddesses for certain, gods, apparitions, ghosts, hobgoblins, phantoms, and spectres visited the great warriors and philosophers of ancient days, why may they not also visit me, who surpass all mortals both in the invincible strength of my arm, and the magnificent gifts of intellect!"

Scarcely had this sublime thought turned itself over in my mind, when I heard a low sound floating upon the air, in tones as gentle as the Æolian Harp, and immediately I recognised it as a spiritual Confederate snort.

" *O Deus Confœderatus, certe!*" I exclaimed, " be thou a spirit of health or a Yankee damned; bring with thee airs from heaven or blasts from Boston ; be thy intents wicked or charitable, thou comest in such questionable shape that I will speak to thee! I'll call thee—Macpherson, Confederate Royal Blower!"

" I am," responded the as yet Unseen, " *the Phantom Confederate, or the Ghost of Madisonville,* doomed for a certain space to walk the night, and by day confined to fast on mule's meat, until the surrender of the garrison shall ensure us Yankee rations! List, list, Oh list!—if ever thou didst thy dear Confederate love—"

Macpherson—" Oh heaven !"

Phantom Confederate—"Then give me thy canteen ; for now am I consumed by devouring thirst !"

Mac.—"Thirst ?"

P. C.—"Ay, thirst most dry, as in the best it is ; but this most dry, queer, and unnatural !"

Mac.—" Haste me to know it, that I, with wings as swift as meditation or the thoughts of love, may swoop to my revenge !"

I then seized the canteen in a glow of generosity, placed the muzzle to my lips, and drank the contents at a single gulp, after which I gave him my canteen as he had requested. " Behold !" I said to him, " the

8

generosity of a true Confederate. Thus did the Louisiana Secesh Convention of 1861 gobble up the Custom-house, Mint, light-houses, arsenal, and revenue cutters of the United States, while Honest Old Abe stood looking on, greedily begrudging the same! Approach, dread corse! that I may gaze upon thee! Is it not enough that the whole Yankee race should be leagued together against me, that spirits must be summoned from the vasty deep, to disturb the repose of the great Confederate warrior?"

The ghost then approached, and, turning my eyes upon him, I beheld a being of majestic mien, dressed in a gray uniform, with a cadaverous countenance, and very dirty. His garments were tattered and torn in such a manner that whenever he stepped, the legs of his breeches released his limbs to the gaze of the midnight Moon.

"Wherefore," I asked, "presumest thou, thus ragged, to come into the presence of a Major General of Confederate Volunteers?"

"Because," replied the ghost, "I haven't got any other clothes. I am the representative phantom of the Southern Confederacy. I was born in South Carolina, and have relatives in eleven States, besides New York city and Vallandigham's district." He then showed me a neck-tie with eleven stars in it, emblematic of the Bonnie Blue Flag, and wrought by the ladies of New Orleans. As he was showing this to me, he smote his head with pain, raised his eyes upwards and exclaimed. "Oh!"

"What's the row, sweety?" I enquired.

"That," replied he, "is occasioned by a contraction

of the Federal lines; I feel it squeezing the brains out of their natural channels."

"Fear not," I answered, "you have not brains enough to suffer serious damage."

Suddenly the Phantom began to dance with the wildest joy, while his whole ghastly face became lighted up with enthusiastic bliss. "Tell me," I said, "the cause of this sudden revulsion of feeling, which seems to have lifted you from the lowest sub-basement of Despair to the highest attic of Delight?"

"A great victory in Pennsylvania!" he replied. "The field of Gettysburg fills me with unspeakable happiness!"

As he spoke, however, I noticed that one of his eyes had been gouged out, and one side of his face completely smashed in, while a stream of blood was coursing to the earth. I inquired the meaning of this, and he replied it was the result of casualties at Gettysburg. "No great victory," he said, "is ever won without appalling sacrifices of life and limb; but Lee has succeeded in getting out of Pennsylvania, with a loss of only forty-five thousand men!"

"Is that all?" I asked.

"Every bit, sure as you live, Macpherson!" cried the Confederate Ghost; and, jumping up, I began to whistle the air of "*Molly, put the kettle on,*" and then, seizing each other's hands, we danced a compound double-shuffle for thirty minutes, in honor of Gettysburg. This magnificent exhibition was interrupted by twinges of excruciating pain, which caused the Ghost to writhe and swear like a man with the gout. "What now?" I enquired.

"That disease," he answered, "is known in the Confederacy as '*Rosecrans in the Legs.*' Whenever a Confederate General gets that disorder, he starts off at a double-quick, and cannot stop until he falls, out of wind. I've got the disease!" he cried, with a tone of terror. "I caught it in Tennessee and Pennsylvania. Curse those malarious Yankee dens of death and perdition!" And so exclaiming, the Ghost started off, and ran so smartly that even I, fleet of limb as I am, could scarcely keep up. Over the blasted heath, through the silent streets of Madisonville, down the lane, and around the dilapidated hospitable abode, ran the fleet-footed Ghost, with Macpherson at his heels. The Idiotic Boy jumped out of bed, and joined in the chase, without waiting to dress. In vain did we try to tree him—in vain to intercept him! To run, run, run, now and forever, seemed to be the strong passion that possessed his Soul, and bound his body obedient to the Will. "Tullahoma!" he cried, as he leaped a wide ditch. "Chattanooga!" he screamed, as he jumped a fence, and fell on the other side, exhausted and apparently defunct. Raising him to his feet, I rubbed his head with a shoe brush until the left eye opened, his lips quivered, and he faintly whispered in my ear the word "Bragg-adocio!"

A Strange Phenomenon.

Now it was that a most extraordinary phenomenon presented itself to my eyes. The Ghost, starting up, suddenly leaped in the air like a bullet-pierced Indian, and fell to the earth in two pieces. Upon examination,

I discovered that he had been clean split in two length-wise, as even and slick as though an immense razor, dropped with the accuracy of a guillotine and the power of Hercules, had severed him in twain. It extended to the top of the cranium. One piece was, in short, the right half of a human body, and the other the left half. It now became doubtful whether consciousness would ever return; but return it did, and each separate part began to talk on its own hook, the left part saying his name was J. Davis, and the right that his name was Magruder Lubbock. The conversation of the two was so incoherent and contradictory, it was evident neither side knew what the other was about, and both bled so copiously that I was in constant fear of instantaneous dissolution. I asked J. Davis to give me the name of this extraordinary disease, and he replied that it was called "*Open Mississippi River*," in the Confederacy. "When a man gets this disorder," he continued, "his case is incurable; there is no possibility of ever again uniting his disjointed parts. I caught it at Vicksburg and Port Hudson, and there is no medicine in the world that can do me good!"

Visit to New Orleans.

The Idiotic Boy and myself tore up a Confederate blanket, and with the pieces tied together the two parts the best we could, and all three of us started for New Orleans in a butcher's cart. As if wonders would never cease, when we arrived in front of the St. Charles Hotel, I found that half of the Ghost had disappeared. On enquiring of the remaining half what had become

of his fellow, he replied that on drawing up before the
Hotel, the right eye had espied General Weitzel standing on the steps, and had immediately left for Texas,
procuring a new crutch at Brashear City.

Curiously did I watch the movements of the remaining half of the Phantom Confederate. He strayed leis-
urely down to the Clay Monument, and informed the
crowd that foreign intervention was now a fixed fact,
and that a French fleet was about to be sent to New
Orleans, in obedience to the petition of our French citizens to the Emperor, through their consul here, to be
protected against a negro insurrection that broke out
in this city on the Fourth of July, and has been raging
with terrible fury ever since. Having made all his
friends in that neighborhood happy, by this announcement, he then walked up to Carondelet-street and visited the Cussed Fool, who read Vallandigham's second
letter aloud from the balcony, to an admiring audience.
At this stage of the proceedings an Extra Era announced the total suppression of the great Confederate
Revolution in New York city, whereupon the Phantom put on a look of dismay, and disappeared through
the back door, in a sudden and unaccountable manner.
I have not seen him since.

Let no one question the literal truth of my ghost
story. I give the world the untarnished honor of a
Confederate soldier and a chivalric Southern gentleman,
that every word I have written is exact, literal truth.

Yours, intermittently,

JAMES D. MACPHERSON.

CHAPTER XXI.

MACPHERSON IS ARRESTED FOR ASSAULT AND BATTERY.—HE
EXPOUNDS THE LAW OF RESPONSIBILITY.—HE VISITS PORT
HUDSON AND VICKSBURG.—HE TESTS THE HOMŒOPATHIC
PRINCIPLE, AND IS CHASED BY THE DEVIL, ETC., ETC.

NOTE.—The Author takes the liberty of introducing an extract
from a very complimentary introduction to the main portion of the
following letter from the Indianapolis *Journal*, as explanatory of its
spirit.

"The responsibility of the 'Abolitionist' for the beating Macpherson gave the 'nigger,' is exactly that which the Copperheads
fasten upon the people of the North for the Southern rebellion. 'If
you had only done what the South wanted,' they say, 'there would
have been no war. Why didn't you get down on your knees and lick
the dust, and take your kicking kindly, as we did, and wanted you to
do? If you had, this unnatural and unconstitutional war would
never have happened. You are responsible for it. The blood is all
on your skirts, you mean, cowardly whelps.' Macpherson epitomizes
the speech of Judge Perkins before the K. G. C.'s last winter 'to a
dot.' The judge, himself, could not state its main point and spirit
better."

MADISONVILLE, LA.,
August 22d, 1863.

SIR :—As I was going along Rampart street, in New
Orleans, last Wednesday, I met a nigger on one side of
the street and an Abolitionist on the other. "Abo.," I
said, "you go over and pull that nigger's wool."

"What for?" asked Abo.

"Because I tell you to," I replied.

"It wouldn't be right," replied Abo.; "the boy has
done me no harm, and I shan't pull his wool."

"If you don't do it," I replied, "I'll knock him down
and pound him within an inch of his life."

"I *shan't* do it," said Abo.; "and I would like to know what he has done to you."

"Nothing," I replied, "but he's a nigger, and that's enough. If you'll pull his wool I'll let him off. But you won't, and if I whip him to death, you'll be responsible for it, you vile inhuman, Abolition renegade! Where's your humanity for the nigger? Where's your philanthropy? Where's your regard for human rights and liberties? The owner and overseer are the only true friends of the nigger! I implore you to save him from the awful mauling I'll give him; but you won't, you infernal, hypocritical, sneaking, puritanical, drawling, damned Massachusetts, Boston, round-head Yankee Abolition fool!" Saying which, with a stream of fire flashing from both eyes, I rushed upon the darkey with the ferocity of a tiger, knocked him flat on his back, kicked his face into a jelly, and whipped him with a raw-hide until he wasn't able to stand on his feet, and a stream of blood ran from every vein in his body.

"What's you gone an' done, massa?" said the unhappy wretch, when I let up on him.

"I, you black numbskull!" I answered; "*I* didn't do it: it was that sneaking Abolition nigger-thief that did it. I am your best friend and protector!"

A policeman came up and arrested me for assault and battery. I was arraigned at the bar as a criminal, and made the following address to the Court:

Macpherson's eloquent Plea in Defense.

"May it please the Court: I do not suppose any thing I can say will alter your predetermined decision, or

your fixed resolution to offer me up as a sacrifice to
Abolition fanaticism. As Socrates stood up to be tried
by a pack of heathen numbskulls, so do I stand up in
the presence of Yankee nincompoops, who no more
comprehend and understand the rules and regulations
of Confederate Courts of Justice, than Jeff. Davis com-
prehends the meaning of his own proclamations. And
as Socrates fell a prey to the lubberheadedness of the
popular Athenian tribunal, so shall I fail, with all my
learning, to prevent this besotted Court from commit-
ting Scandalum Magnatum—an offense against Confederate prelates and dignitaries, which, under the old
statutes of England, was no offense when committed
against common folks, but a crime when done to big
men like me. Nevertheless, if the truth can permeate
your bestial intellects, allow me to call your attention
to the law of this case. In the first place, I take the
ground that the authority of Governor Moore and the
Louisiana Legislature (which at last accounts was in
session behind the Rocky Mountains), is in force in this
city, and that the Black Code of Louisiana is binding
upon Yankees who come into the Department of the
Gulf. I also plead the usages and customs of the Confederates in justification of my conduct; and this
brings me to a logical analysis of the case. The witnesses against me are two—a nigger and an Abolitionist. Under the Black Code of Louisiana, a slave's
testimony cannot be taken in a Court of Justice, and
under the former precedents and usages of this great
Confederate Commonwealth, an Abolitionist should be
hung without trial. Therefore, the nigger's evidence
is no evidence at all, and the Abolitionist has no busi-

ness here; he had better go North and sing psalms, and not venture into my Department, for if he does I'll hang him higher than Haman or John Brown. I therefore ask the Court to discharge me, send the nigger back to Confederate slavery, and hang the Abolitionist."

The Court didn't see it, and so I continued my thrilling discourse:

"In the second place, the Abolition Cuss is responsible for the pounding of the darkey; since, had he pulled his wool as I requested him to do, I should not have touched the black brute. But Horace Greeley is the author of this war, and Wendell Phillips got up the late riots in New York, as I can prove to you by an editorial in one of the New Orleans papers: and what can you expect of an Abolitionist any how? They alone are responsible for the war and for slavery, and therefore I ought to be discharged."

In spite of this irresistible logic, which should have secured my instant release, the Court declined to let me off, and was about to pronounce sentence, when I jumped out of the second-story window, and made off for Madisonville so fast that the whole Department of the Gulf couldn't catch me.

Macpherson visits Port Hudson and Vicksburg.

I went up to Port Hudson and Vicksburg on the steamer Crescent, with a whole load of Yankee generals, colonels, congressmen, lawyers, and editors, and shed tears of inconsolable grief as I gazed upon the deserted Confederate rat-holes behind the parapets of Port Hud-

son, where we stopped to look at the works. Not
believing that the place had been taken, I enquired for
the headquarters of General Gardner, and was directed to an old house that had many holes through the
roof, and the balcony clean knocked off by Yankee
shells.

"Is General Gardner in?" I enquired of a sentinel.

"Yes," was the reply, "he is in jail."

I knew then that Port Hudson was taken, and so
telegraphed to the Cussed Fool of Carondelet street. I
regret to add that my observations at Vicksburg were
equally unsatisfactory.

Similia Similibus Curantur.

Heart-sick and discouraged at the drooping condition
of the Confederate cause on the Mississippi, I returned
to Madisonville, and devoted myself wholly to drinking. Having swallowed one demijohn of Louisiana
Rum, I became beastly drunk ; and then it was that the
great principle of Hahnemann—"like cures like"—burst
upon my mind. If it be true, I thought, that like
cures like, then will another demijohn of the same destructive liquid restore my mind and body to their accustomed activity. Accordingly I applied the remedy
in doses larger than those which had produced the
disease, and it resulted in a perfect cure. I got over
being drunk, but in doing so I got the delirium tre-
mens, which lasted me for two weeks, and confined me
to my room. That is the reason I have not written
any letters recently.

I never suspected that the Devil was a hod-carrier

until I was prostrated by this singular disorder; but as
soon as the thing was fairly on me, I saw him with a hod
of bricks on the top of his head, grinning at me hideous-
ly, and every now and then picking out a brick and
pitching it at my head with unerring aim. I cut around
the house because the Devil was after me, but he was
too fast, and hit me at every step. He was dressed in
gray uniform, a good deal soiled and faded, and his
shoes had burst out so that it showed his cloven foot.
This performance continued at intervals for fourteen
days, and whenever the Old Boy chased me around the
house, he hummed the following:

DITTY, SUNG BY OLD SCRATCH AS HE CHASED MACPHER-
SON WITH BRICKS.

Dear Jeff.'s sick they say,
But I mean he shall stay
On earth a while longer;
My cause will be stronger
With his plotting you see;
So a while let him be!

Secession I like,
It was a ten-strike;
My clerks are all busy—
Writing names till they're dizzy!
Yet awhile, it is planned,
Jeff.'s card-house shall stand!   '

I like men that lie
So much faster than I
Ever could, I believe,
E'en in dealing with Eve!
Yes, the Rebs *are* a wonder,
They lie so like thunder!

I love New York rioters
And slung-shot proprietors,
Who'll burn an Asylum;
Not yet will I "spile" 'em!

I've suspended my orders
To bring 'em into my borders!

The Copperhead faction
Suits me just to a fraction,
They follow Fernando
And play to my hand so,
And never pull triggers
But in shooting poor niggers!

And as for that standing sham,
Mr. Vallandigham,
And New York Judge McCunn,
There never was better one;
They preach habeas corpus
And blow like a porpoise!

Yet a while let 'em hobble,
But soon will I gobble
The whole, as guerillas
Seize chickens or fillies,
With greater momentum
Than grape could have sent 'em!

When he finished up the performance of this ditty, he disappeared, and I arose clothed and in my right mind.

Yours, occasionally,
J. BUCHANAN MACPHERSON.

CHAPTER XXII.

**MACPHERSON IS SEIZED WITH THE NEWSPAPER MANIA, AND DE-
TERMINES TO BECOME AN EDITOR.—HE DISSOLVES THE ARMY
OF MADISONVILLE, ETC., ETC.**

NOTE.—At the time this letter was published, a great number of
newspaper schemes were on foot in New Orleans. No less than three
new dailies were in contemplation, beside one which had actually
been started.

MADISONVILLE, LA.,
Oct. 9, 1863.

SIR:—Returning from the Convention of General
Magruder and the kicked-out Governors, recently held
in Texas, I stopped in New Orleans on my return. But
I soon discovered that a malignant and destructive contagion had broken out in that city, which, in its devas-
tating ravages, spared neither age, sex, color, nor condition. From the high in position down to the lowest
son of a gun, it took all, sparing none in its onward and
miraculous progress. As the hot and noxious simoom
sweeps over the burning sand, while a thick sulphurous
exhalation rises from the earth, first in hurried gyra-
tions, and then ascends the air and covers the whole
heavens—while hissing and crackling noises are heard,
and animal life perishes as though touched by Greek
fire, even so had this pestilent epidemic seized with an
unyielding grasp every one who ventured within the
circle of its magic influence. The millionaire was taken
in the midst of luxury and splendor; the lawyer in his
office; the literati in garrets; fair women fell its vic-

tims; even a Confederate, fresh from Fort Jackson, was stricken before he had been three days from prison.

My first impulse was to skedaddle, as unceremoniously as the Reliable Gentleman of the St. Charles Hotel did, when he heard there was a case of yellow fever in town. But learning that the disease seldom proved fatal, except to the pocket, I determined to take my chances, especially as I had no money, and was, in fact, a travelling object of charity. But I had not been in the city two hours before I was seized with a violent and uncontrollable desire to start a daily newspaper, or to get an interest in one already started. It came upon me like a flash of lightning hurled by the hand of Jupiter, when he darts the destructive bolts from the summit of divine Olympus; and it worked upon my mind in a manner so violent that I soon fell sprawling on the floor, as flat as one of Sylvanus Cobb's novels. The crash of my fall hastily brought a friend to my side. "Great Heaven!" he exclaimed; "Macpherson has got the contagion! A physician, quick! for the love of Confederate intellect!" A distinguished physician soon appeared, felt of my bounding pulse, and began to question me as to the symptoms of the disorder.

"This desire to start a newspaper," he began—"have you ever had it before?"

"Only in slight degree," I answered him. "For some time I have had it in my head to put the Idiotic Boy in editorial charge of a paper; for the manner in which the press in New Orleans is conducted, has convinced me that he would be a bright and shining light among his cotemporaries. But that was as nothing compared to the desire which I now feel. A wild,

restless fatality, an irresistible purpose, consume me,
as if one of Gillmore's batteries had been opened,
sweeping Greek Fire through my bones."

"There is no doubt as to what ails you," said the
good Doctor, shaking his head gravely; "you have
caught the prevailing distemper, known in medical
parlance as the Newspaper Mania!"

"Is there no remedy!" I asked.

"Only one that I know of," he answered.

"And what might that be?" I inquired.

"To pay the bills of some newspaper establishment
for a month," he replied, "receiving in return the receipts of the concern, has, so far as my observation
goes, proved an effectual remedy for all complaints of
this nature."

"Is the remedy severe?" I asked.

"Alas! yes," he answered; "none but millionaires
can indulge in it; and unless you have plenty of
metal, your case is hopeless."

I therefore hurried back to Madisonville, hoping that
a change of climate and the quiet repose of my home,
might restore my mental equilibrium; or that, con-
certing measures with the Honest Jew, I might gratify
the terrible desire that now burned to the very mar-
row of my bones.

Imagine my horror, therefore, when on reaching my
abode, I found that the very disorder from which I
had hoped to escape, was raging with tenfold fury in
Madisonville. The Idiotic Boy, first among the vic-
tims, had already started a daily, and was astonishing
the human race with the wisdom and genius of his
leaders. Three secret prospectuses were in circulation

for rival sheets; and even the military had not escaped
the distemper. The whole Buzz-Saw Division had
turned job-printers, and every stationer and bookseller
in town was printing posters. I asked the Honest
Jew, how much the average profits of a newspaper
were; and he answered with glowing eyeballs, that a
daily newspaper made a hundred thousand dollars
every three days; and that it was his intention to set
two running at once, in a large building fronting on
two streets—a newspaper at each end. Both, he said,
could be printed from the same form, and as the public
would never read either, they would not discover the
base deception.

"The press of Madisonville is already large," I began; "its papers, in fact, are more numerous than its
readers; and if we are to establish a new concern, or
seize an old one, we must advocate some principle that
nobody believed, or ever can believe; so that ours will
be the exclusive organ of that Idea, and meet with no
competition."

"Vat brinciple do you call dat?" enquired the Israelite.

"That," I replied, "is yet to be evolved from the
Mammoth Brain of him now before you; it is a question of intellect that I alone can solve."

"I have him!" said the Jew.

"What is it?" I asked.

"No brinciple!" he replied, with a look of triumph.
"Brinciple be tampt! Bublish a baper mit no brinciple at all."

But the great Idea, I saw, was Consolidation. I
would buy or seize all the newspaper establishments

in Madisonville; all their presses, all their types. I
would then construct a building of gigantic propor-
tions, eighteen stories high and five thousand feet
front on four streets, and into this magnificent temple
of art should be put all the materials of all the offices
in this city; and my great mind and overshadowing
genius should be the ruling and guiding spirit of the
splendid whole. All rival factions would then bow to
me, and all give me their patronage. The lion should
lie down with the lamb, the Confederate with the
Yankee, the tiger with the jackass, the elephant with
the baboon, and the greatest man of the age should
lead them. Filled with this Idea, even as my insides
were filled with liquid Rum, I arose and issued the
following:

General Order No. 0.

HEADQUARTERS,
DEPARTMENT OF MADISONVILLE,
Madisonville, La., Oct. 1st, 1863.

The General Commanding announces that the Army of Madisonville is hereby dissolved. The men have fought bravely without
pay, and I should consider it an insult to their pride and patriotism to offer them money in this late stage of their protracted de-
privations and sufferings. They will, therefore, be immediately
mustered out of the service without further compensation than the
consciousness of having done their duty, and of having served
under the greatest warrior of ancient or modern times. The
money which would have been paid to the troops under different
circumstances, will be turned over to the Honest Jew, who will
disburse the same in accordance with verbal instructions from
these Headquarters. Soldiers of the Department of Madisonville!
your swords shall be beaten into printing presses, and your bayonets into ink-rollers; no more shall you grapple with bloody
foes, but you shall stick type and do job printing. But, under all
circumstances, you will be cheered by the grateful reflection that
your General will retain his rank and pay, whether sweating

blood on the field of carnage, or swaying the destinies of the human race with the editorial pen.

By command of MAJOR GENERAL JAMES B. MACPHERSON.

THE IDIOTIC BOY, Chief of Staff.

Thus, Consolidation and the downfall of all rivalry is the grand Idea that now possesses me. I shall exchange the gray gory garments of war for the editorial robe, and shall make my paper the organ of every principle and sentiment known to mankind. I shall take one position in one article and follow it immediately by another, taking a directly opposite view; and thus will I be able to conciliate all conflicting opinions and interests. Farewell the plumed troop and the big wars that make ambition virtue! Oh, farewell the braying mule and the shrill trumpet, the ear-piercing fife, the Confederate flag, and all the pride, pomp, and circumstance of glorious war—except the pay! And oh, you mortal Confederate engines, whose rude throats the immortal Jove's dread clamors poorly counterfeit, Farewell!—Macpherson's occupation's changed!

Yours, undeviatingly,

JAMES B. MACPHERSON.

CHAPTER XXIII.

MACPHERSON, DISGUSTED WITH THE NEWSPAPER BUSINESS, RE-
SOLVES TO ACQUIRE OFFICE AND CIVIL RENOWN.—THE
RESTORATION OF CIVIL GOVERNMENT IN LOUISIANA.—MAC-
PHERSON IS ELECTED GOVERNOR OF THE STATE, ETC., ETC.

NOTE.—The pro-slavery party of Louisiana, hoping to retain the
"divine institution" in New Orleans and other parishes where it was
not abolished by the President's Proclamation, formed a scheme to
hold an election on the second day of November, 1863, the day fixed by
the old Constitution, for a Governor, Congressmen, State officers, and
a Legislature. Of course there could have been no legality or authority in such an election, since it had not been called by the Governor, or countenanced in any manner by the military authorities.
The State officers who were in Louisiana previous to the outbreak
of the rebellion, had deserted their posts and joined the Confederacy ; and the only government in Louisiana, since the occupation
of New Orleans by the United States forces, has been the military
government. A few Copperheads—perhaps twenty, all told—met
secretly in Masonic Hall, and nominated candidates for the different
offices. Their proceedings and designs were kept profoundly secret,
as long as possible. They determined that on the Wednesday pre-
ceding the election, they would issue a call for a mass-meeting, to
be held the next Saturday evening, to ratify their nominations. In
other words, the people were to have *five days'* notice before the
election. The matter "leaked out," however, a little sooner than
the conspirators intended to have it. But on the Wednesday pre-
ceding the day fixed for the election, the Masonic Hall clique issued
an "Address to the People of Louisiana," calling upon them to convene at the usual places of voting, the next Monday, and elect civil
officers, and assuring them there was "nothing to prevent" it ; that
the military would not interfere, and that this course would meet the
approval of the national government. "On the second of November,
then," said the address, "go to the polls and cast your votes as usual ;
your chosen Congressmen will take their seats on the first Monday of
December ; your chosen Legislators will meet on the third Monday
of January and organise ; your State officers will on the same day be

Inaugurated, and thus the wheels of civil government will be once
more set in motion in our State, and we trust prosperously and for
the benefit of mankind. Fail to make this little effort, and your last
opportunity for renewing Civil State Government, in accordance
with legal provisions, will fruitlessly pass, with the probable destruction of Republican Institutions. * * *

"Let us arise, then, and go forth and perform the imperative and
sacred duty of electing the officers of a Civil Government in Louisiana, on *Monday, the second day of November*, the time appointed by
our laws; and if we fail, it may be the last time we will have the
power of acting as freemen."

The purpose of this movement, it was well understood, was to restore the infamous Black Code of Louisiana—a code most barbarous
in its provisions—and to re-establish slavery on its former foundations. But the scheme, as soon as it was exposed, subjected its
authors to such ridicule and contempt, that they "backed out" of it,
and published an announcement that the election would not be held,
since it was feared that the people would not vote! But the end it
seems was not yet; for the gentlemen who were nominated by Masonic
Hall, had the assurance to claim that they were entitled to exercise
the offices for which they were named, on the ground that *had the
election been held*, they would have received a majority of the votes!
Nearly all the men nominated by Masonic Hall for State officers
were residents of New Orleans. Some of them were notorious for
their rebel proclivities; some had signed or voted for the Ordinance
of Secession, in the Convention of 1861.

MADISONVILLE, LA.,
October 30th, 1863.

SIR :—As the Devil, after the great secession movement described by Milton, was hurled headlong flam-
ing from the ethereal sky, with hideous ruin and com-
bustion, down to bottomless perdition, there to dwell
in adamantine chains and penal fire, so had I been
pitched heels over head from the lofty position I once
occupied, and was nowhere. The few days' experience
I had in the newspaper business came near worrying
the life out of me. Every five minutes during the
night, my door-bell would ring furiously, and some
new candidate for newspaperial fame and wealth would

present himself, with propositions to buy me out at half price or to steal the concern outright, until finally in disgust I told the Honest Jew to take the whole concern and go to the devil with it, or anywhere else, provided he would give me an hour's sleep.

Having disbanded the army of Madisonville, and the Buzz-Saw Division having all turned job printers, I have felt my powers sensibly decline. I turned my attention to philosophy, which is a good thing in its way; but even Socrates was as poor as a Confederate pack-horse, and was abused for it by his wife. In short, philosophy don't pay bills. Therefore, having lost military power, I determined to acquire enough civil grandeur to make up for it; and I planned a grand scheme for inaugurating civil government in Louisiana. Secresy was very important, since the plot was one so wise that the lubberly-headed masses of the people could never comprehend or appreciate it. Therefore, I called a meeting of the faithful in the attic of my dilapidated hospitable abode, to lay before them the splendid conception that had sprung from my Mammoth Brain. The better to ensure secresy, a grip and pass-word were adopted. The grip consisted of a grab at the nasal organ, and the pass-word was: "*Treasury.*" The following distinguished statesmen were present :

James Buchanan Macpherson, the Confederate Philosopher and Southern Blower; his son, and Chief of Staff, the Idiotic Boy; his Quartermaster, the Honest Jew; his Commissary, the Unhappy Cuss; his Chief of Cavalry, the Solitary Horseman; his Chief of Artillery, the Inconsolable Thug; his Chief of Signal Corps, the Southern Source; his Judge Advocate, the Weep-

ing Orphan; his Aids-de-Camp, the Macedonian, the
Reliable Gentleman, and the Cussed Fool of Carondelet-
street.

It was a touching sight, and one calculated to bring
tears to the eyes of an alligator, to look upon this assembly of fallen greatness. Every man of them had
enjoyed a fat office under me in the days of my martial
glory; but now they looked like a set of darned loafers,
with lank jaws and seedy breeches. They reminded
me of the congregation of registered enemies that Satan
got around him in the infernal regions, after his repulse
by the heavenly army. I arose and addressed them
as follows:

Macpherson's Address.

"Fellow-citizens of Louisiana! We address you as
loyal to the Government." [A voice: "Which Government?"] *Macpherson:* "None of your d—d business,
you hounds! Wait till my scheme is put into execution, and then learn what it is by the results. As loyal
citizens you have duties to perform to me and yourselves, your State and country. We are in danger, and
immediate action is required. The fact is, you are like
me in one respect—you all want office; and the want
of civil government in our State can, by a proper effort
on your part, soon be supplied, under laws and a Constitution formed and adopted by yourselves, in a time
of profound peace. It is made your duty as well as
your right, to meet at the usual places, and cast your
votes for me as Governor, and for yourselves to fill the
best offices in the State. Heretofore in our history the
direction of these elections has been had by legal

agents; but the legal agents now have no authority of
any sort, and, therefore, we will take charge of the
whole business ourselves. We held a State election in
1861, and nothing has since happened that amounts to
any thing. We promise you that the military will not
interfere, there being none in this part of the country;
and we think we can assure you that your action in
this respect will meet the approval of the National Government." [A voice : " Which National Government ?"]
Macpherson : " Dry up, you vagabond ! We urge upon
you *action* in this important crisis. It will convince
the world of our wish and determination to manage the
offices of the State and the public revenue in the manner most satisfactory to ourselves; it will encourage all
desirous of making a splurge in other States, and will
have a tendency to cause the soldiers to throw down
their arms, and give us our own way, overawed by the
civil grandeur that will surround us. Go to the polls
then ! Your Governor will assume his constitutional
functions, and the Legislature will convene in Madi
sonville forthwith; your Congressmen will take their
seats as soon as they can find them." [A voice: " In
Washington or in Richmond ?"]

Macpherson : " Silence, you low-lived scoundrel !
It is our intention to assume our old status, in order
that we can clear the State of Yankee office-holders,
and whip our niggers under our own vine and fig-tree,
with none to molest or to make us afraid. Let us
arise, then, and go forth and perform the imperative
and sacred duty of electing ourselves to office; and if
we fail, it may be the last time we shall have the
power of acting as freemen—that is, thrashing the

niggers and spending the public fund according to our own discretion!"

At the conclusion of this able and patriotic address, a burst of applause greeted me like the roar of battle.

The Southern Source then arose, and stated that he had just had an interview with Jeff. Davis, and had been assured of his approval and support. The Emperor of France had also promised a land and naval force to co-operate with the new governor. [Applause.]

The Idiotic Boy was loudly called for, but declined to speak, as he was about to be a candidate for the suffrages of his fellow-citizens for one of the highest offices in their gift. Modesty, he said, prevented him addressing the audience; but he nevertheless went on and spoke two columns, saying that the facts of secession and rebellion had changed nothing, except to turn the offices over to the present company, which he believed to be a good thing. In conclusion, he expressed the hope that the advertising and job work necessary to be done, would be given to the paper with which it was well known he was connected. [Hisses by the Honest Jew and other publishers.] I interfered, saying, that the newspaper business had played out, and had nothing to do with political questions.

The Honest Jew said: "Pefore I gives mine subbort of der measure, I vish to know if I be made Dreasurer. You makes me Dreasurer, I zteals the bublic funds and tivides mit you vun half the brofit!" [Applause, and the nomination of the Honest Jew as State Treasurer by acclamation.]

The meeting then proceeded to nominate candidates, when the following ticket was agreed to:

9

STATE ELECTION.

For Governor:
JAMES BUCHANAN MACPHERSON,
Of Madisonville.

For Lieutenant Governor:
THE IDIOTIC BOY,
Of Madisonville.

For Secretary of State:
THE UNHAPPY CUSS,
Of Madisonville.

For State Treasurer:
THE HONEST JEW,
Of Madisonville.

For Auditor:
THE RELIABLE GENTLEMAN,
Of Madisonville.

For Attorney General:
THE WEEPING ORPHAN,
Of Madisonville.

For Superintendent of Public Education:
THE SOUTHERN SOURCE,
Of Madisonville.

For Congress—Madisonville District:
THE CUSSED FOOL,
Of Madisonville.

For Congress—State at Large:
THE SOLITARY HORSEMAN,
Of Madisonville.

It was suggested that Madisonville was not properly
represented on the ticket. We had the ballots printed

immediately, and to each one was attached the following:

Notice.—Gentlemen wishing to become members of the State Senate and Legislature, can be accommodated by paying their initiation fee and becoming members of the patriotic association that manufactured the above ticket. As soon as the party is large euongh, a candidate will be named for each district in the State.

J. B. M., Governor

Grand Ratification Meeting.

It was voted unanimously that time was of great consequence, and that the sooner we were elected the surer we would be of our offices. Wishing, however, to give the lubberly-headed people a fair show, we called a grand Ratification Meeting, to be held at Merritt's Hotel, in Madisonville, the next morning at five o'clock.

The sun was not up when the assembly convened, but that made no difference. On motion, James B. Macpherson, of Madisonville, was chosen President; and the Idiotic Boy, of Madisonville, was appointed Secretary. A list of Vice-Presidents was then appointed as follows: The Unhappy Cuss, of Madisonville; the Honest Jew, of Madisonville; the Reliable Gentleman, of Madisonville; the Weeping Orphan, of Madisonville; the Southern Source, of Madisonville; the Cussed Fool, of Madisonville; the Solitary Horseman, of Madisonville.

The audience consisted of the Inconsolable Thug, of Madisonville, the bar-keeper of Merritt's Madisonville Hotel (drunk), and three niggers of Madisonville, sleeping on the sidewalk.

"Fellow-citizens of Louisiana!" I said, "I am thank-

ful for the honor conferred upon me, in being called to
preside over the deliberations of this great assembly.
I am happy to greet my fellow-citizens of Louisiana
upon this auspicious occasion. [Three cheers by the
Inconsolable Thug, who knocked down the barkeeper,
by way of a 'tiger.'] Our principles are well known.
We go for restoring the State as it was before the Yankee brutes came down here and took New Orleans; and
we believe that the offices of a State belong to the
great men of the State. If elected to the office of Governor by the suffrages of the people, I shall perform the
duties of the office in a manner perfectly satisfactory
to myself." [Applause on the platform.]

The Idiotic Boy suggested that the ticket had been
enthusiastically endorsed by the people of Louisiana,
and that the election ought to come off at six o'clock the
same morning. We therefore adjourned to the usual
places of holding elections, and in fifteen minutes thereafter the polls closed. The result was proclaimed
in a loud tone of voice, and it was found that every
candidate nominated in the attic had been elected without opposition.

The only disturbance at the polls was occasioned by
the Inconsolable Thug, who rolled up his coat and
pulled off his sleeves, and fought the barkeeper and
the niggers for the drinks.

At seven o'clock A. M. of the same day, I was solemnly
inaugurated Governor of the State of Louisiana. The
ceremonies were performed at Merritt's Hotel, Madisonville. A high stool was arranged in front of the
bar, with a decanter and glass within reach; and on
this stool I took my seat, looking as wise as though I

had had my head soaked in sage tea for four months; while on my left was the Lieutenant-Governor elect and the other State dignitaries. The oath was administered by the barkeeper, after which I delivered the following Inaugural Address:

"Fellow-citizens of Louisiana! It is customary on occasions of the solemn inauguration of the Chief Magistrate of the State, that his predecessor should be present. But in the present instance I am authorised to say that it is not convenient for Governor Moore to attend. I beg leave to say that I shall pursue the same policy that he did, and I sincerely pray that my gubernatorial career may be crowned with results no less brilliant than those he realised."

Amid the plaudits of the crowd, I was then escorted to the D. II. Abode, now become the Executive Mansion, amid salvos of artillery from a hundred-pound wooden howitzer. I rode on a triumphal horse-car decorated with old newspapers and drawn by eight jackasses. The officers of State having been sworn in, I issued the following:

PROCLAMATION

TO THE PEOPLE OF LOUISIANA.

I, James Buchanan Macpherson, having been unanimously elected Governor of the State of Louisiana, hereby issue this my Proclamation, and decree as follows:

1. That the State House at Baton Rouge having been burned down, the seat of Government is removed to Madisonville, where the Legislature will convene at one o'clock this afternoon.

2. The salaries of all public officers are hereby doubled, and a year's salary shall be drawn in advance.

3. The public debt having increased beyond the capacity of the

treasury, the same is hereby cancelled, and the State Treasurer will rub out and begin anew.

4. The Confederate Arithmetic is hereby designated as the official mathematical system, and the Superintendent of Education will see that none other is taught.

5. Civil government having now been firmly established in the whole of Louisiana, the United States army is directed to pack up and leave by the next steamer for the North; and every damned Yankee found in the State after the second day of November, will be hung to a lamp-post.

    In witness whereof, I have hereunto set the seal of the State of Louisiana, on the twenty-eighth day of October, Anno Domini one thousand eight hundred and sixty-three, and of the Southern Confederacy, three.

By the Governor.

THE UNHAPPY CUSS, Secretary of State.

I will now conclude my epistle, expressing the hope that the life of the undersigned may be prolonged to an unnatural extent, and that he may be re-elected at the expiration of his present term.

Yours, Gubernatorially,

JAMES BUCHANAN MACPHERSON.

CHAPTER XXIV.

The Governor is besieged by Office-seekers.—The ingenious Method by which he dispersed the Mob.—The
True Southern Patriot, and why he would not accept
Office.—The Idiotic Boy chastised.—The Governor
makes a Pilgrimage to Richmond.—The full and authentic History of the Congressional Career of the
Cussed Fool and the Solitary Horseman, etc., etc.

Executive Mansion,
Madisonville, La.,
Dec. 31st, 1863.

Sir:—Since my elevation to the lofty position of
Governor of Louisiana, every Confederate within five
thousand miles of Madisonville has applied to me for
an office. I was delighted beyond measure to see the
amount of patriotism which these faithful sons of chivalry possessed. Every one of them, I found, had first
raised the Confederate flag in New Orleans, and had
been last to pull it down when the infernal Yankees
took possession of that impregnable city. Every one
of them had suffered tenfold persecution, and the ago-
nies of purgatorial punishment for the holy cause of
Southern rights; and there was not one who did not
declare that his soul would swell with gratitude, if I
would point out to him a method in which he might
immediately spend the remnants of his fortune and
pour out his heart's blood for the sacred Confederacy.

How the Governor got rid of 'em.

"Sweet Confederate patriots!" I said, addressing them from the roof of the house; " you all want office. I sympathise with your honorable ambition, and I will give every one of you a position [loud shouts of applause on all sides] on certain terms. [Many voices: 'Give us the terms, Governor!' and, 'We accept.'] Don't be in a hurry about accepting, you hounds! until you hear the conditions. You are all anxious to serve the Confederacy in the most effectual manner. [Cries of 'yes,' 'that's so,' et cetera.] You would willingly lay down your lives, your fortunes, and your sacred honor on the glorious altar of Southern Independence. [Loud cries of 'yes,' and 'bully for the Gov.!'] Well, sweet ones! you shall be accommodated. [Cheers and shouts for fifteen minutes.] Every one of you shall have a posish under my administration, if you will enlist in the Confederate army for three years or during the war, unless sooner discharged!"

A hum of voices was heard on all sides, like that described by Homer, when the Greeks issued from their black ships to pounce upon Priam. It grew fainter and fainter, until it fell upon the ear like strains of distant music, and then it died out altogether. On looking about me, I discovered that the vast assembly of patriots had disappeared. Every mother's son of 'em had skedaddled; not one has since asked for an office or shown his head in Madisonville.

The True Southern Patriot.

I then made the acquaintance of the True Southern Patriot; the man who didn't want office. He was a man of meek manners, and said he only came to assure me of his supreme admiration of my great abilities, and that he was mine respectfully until death should us part. I asked him if he would like to go to Congress, whereupon he seemed stricken with horror. " No," he replied, " the time of my political ambition has passed; nothing on earth would induce me to accept an office."

On questioning him, I found that he already held four offices under the Confederate Government; and to this fact I attributed his reluctance to take a posish.

The Idiotic Boy chastised.

I have prepared my letters to THE ERA for publication in book form, and the manuscript has already gone on to the publisher in New York. It will be the greatest work that ever emanated from the human intellect, and as a history of Confederate Glory will equal in truthfulness the story of Sinbad the Sailor. I gathered all the letters together in a big pile, and taking up a pair of scissors, remarked to the Idiotic Boy that I should cut from them every part not worth printing.

" If you do that," replied the Imbecile Youth. " your book will not make two pages."

I flogged him like Satan for that speech.   But when

I came to look over the letters, I found he was altogether too near the truth, and for this I flogged him again within an inch of his life.

The Governor's Pilgrimage to Richmond.

As the faithful Mohammedans make a pilgrimage to Mecca for the good of the soul, so did I start for Richmond in the search of political power. It will be remembered by the readers of my former able production, that at the time I was elected Governor of Louisiana, a whole set of State officers was chosen, and that the Cussed Fool and the Solitary Horseman were elected as representatives in Congress. The election was held in Madisonville before daylight, on the morning of October 28th, 1863, and the barkeeper of Merritt's Hotel administered the oath of office. It may seem strange that the Chief Magistrate of a great State should be hard up; but such, nevertheless, was the case: for the Treasurer, the Honest Jew, stole all the money, and ran away. I therefore called a council of State, and addressed them as follows:

"Brother dignitaries of the Commonwealth of Louisiana! called, as all of us were, by the unanimous suffrages and sufferings of our fellow-citizens, to uphold the dignity and power of the State, and to dispose of the public revenue according to the dictates of our own consciences, it becomes our duty to stand by the ship of State in adversity as well as in prosperity. Honest poverty has been held as a mark of honor by the wisest sages of antiquity; and if it be in truth an honor, then are we entitled to the highest respect, for there isn't a red in the treasury, and it becomes our duty to raise the wind. Happily, an honorable way is open for the accomplishment of this most desirable object. I have therefore to propose that the Cussed Fool and the Solitary Horseman shall go to Richmond to get seats in Congress, if possible. But for fear they may not succeed, I will go with them, and we will collect mileage from the Sergeant-at-arms, before their claim is passed upon by the House. This will yield a very handsome sum, and we will divide it equally among the various officers of the State."

This proposition was received with loud shouts of approval; and accompanied by the two members of Congress and the Idiotic Boy (Lieutenant Governor), we set out for the great Confederate capital. I journeyed over hills and mountains and through valleys, until I arrived in a big swamp, which, I was told, was formerly known as the Chickahominy Bottoms, but is now called Strategy Swamp, because a whole army got swamped while practising strategy in those gloomy regions. I sank to my middle every time I stepped; and the Idiotic Boy informed me that it only required a siege of the malarious fever to ruin my constitution and complete my military education.

I then debouched from the woods, and, lo and behold! the city of Jeff. Davis loomed upon my vision. "O great Confederate Jerusalem!" I exclaimed, "as all the Honest Jews shall some day be gathered together in Palestine, so shall all the Confederates soon swarm within thy gates, when Meade, Grant, and Gilmore impiously crowd them up in one place. And as the footprint of Mohammed is preserved in a sacred temple, so shall the mark of my Confederate shoes form a shrine for future generations?"

We then advanced to the city by the right flank, and I immediately visited the Executive Mansion, and had an interview with Jeff. Davis. Jeff. was glad to see me, but said he had been a little more near-sighted than usual since Chickamauga. I told him we came as representatives of a great principle.

"What principle is that?" asked Jeff.

"Mileage," I answered.

He said he hoped we would succeed, and that the best plan would be to get the Clerk of the House drunk, and hire him to place the names of the two Congressmen on the roll before any objection was raised; and then to apply immediately to the Sergeant-at-arms for mileage.

It is a melancholy fact that the human mind is so constituted, in some instances, that it is open to the voice of duty and justice only after it has received the inducement of a liberal fee. And it is providential, perhaps, that the Louisiana Delegation had no money; otherwise we might have been tempted to try to bribe the Clerk. But we found this unnecessary. The Clerk was anxious to be re-elected, and in order to accomplish this he determined not to enroll the names of any but those who would vote for him, and a promise to vote for him was all that was needed to secure a place on the roll of members.

The great and momentous day at last arrived for Congress to assemble. The Louisiana Delegation looked pale and haggard, but I told them I would stand by them until they got their mileage. We approached the Sergeant-at-arms, where, in accordance with instructions, the Cussed Fool and the Solitary Horseman foll prostrate before that official dignitary, and in tears and lamentations sufficient to move a house, implored him to pay them their mileage. The Sergeant-at-arms replied that he didn't see it, and I haven't seen it yet myself.

The Louisiana Delegation then arose to its feet, and we all went into the House of Representatives together, when the following proceedings occurred:

Mr. STEVENS said: I ask to have the credentials of the persons claiming to be representatives from Louisiana read.

CLERK (just drunk enough to be funny).—The Clerk will gratify the curiosity of the gentleman. [Laughter by the Idiotic Boy, the Louisiana Delegation, and me.]

Now came the greatest triumph of my life; for the Clerk proceeded to read, in a clear and distinct tone of voice, the credentials which I had prepared by four weeks' labor, and a careful study of Webster's Dictionary and the Black Code of Louisiana:

CREDENTIALS.

I, James Buchanan Macpherson, Governor of the State of Louisiana, duly and legally elected by the voters of said State, in pursuance of my twenty-second letter to the ERA, and the Constitution and laws, and inaugurated by taking the oath administered by the barkeeper of Merritt's Hotel, do certify that at an election begun and held in Madisonville, before daylight, on the morning of the twenty-eighth day of October, 1863, in accordance with Masonic Hall, for the purpose of electing Representatives from said State and raising the wind, the following named persons were regularly elected to represent said State in said Congress for the term of two years from the fourth day of March, 1863, namely:

The Cussed Fool.

The Solitary Horseman.

All of whom were regularly elected in accordance with the Constitution and Laws of said State of Louisiana, as by me construed and interpreted.

In testimony whereof, I, James Buchanan Macpherson, Author of the Confederate Arithmetic, Traveller through the Louisiana Lowlands Low, Clergyman, Poet, Philosopher, Plato of the Confederacy, Warrior, great Southern Blower, and Governor, elected as aforesaid, do hereby commission said persons, so elected as aforesaid and duly sworn, to represent said State in the said Confederate Congress, on condition that they shall pay my hotel bills as long as I remain in Richmond, and divide their mileage with me honorably and justly; and I do hereby give these credentials in evidence of their fair and square election; and I do hereby affix my private seal of office, my predecessor and friend, Moore, having carried off the great seal, and having had no opportunity to send it back, in consequence of General Banks chasing him like the devil last spring, from which he has never recovered; and my said private seal I have hereunto affixed this twentieth day of November, in the third year of Jeff. Davis, and the year of our Lord, 1863.

{ L. S. }   JAMES BUCHANAN MACPHERSON,
                                  Governor of the State of Louisiana.

My private seal, which I affixed to the above document, is the picture of a jackass grabbing at a crib beyond his reach.

Stevens moved to strike the name of the Cussed Fool and the Solitary Horseman from the roll of members; but was induced to withdraw it, and we proceeded to the election of a speaker. The Louisiana Delegation voted for a candidate of their own, and thus succeeded in getting their names in the Congressional proceedings. The future historian, the unborn Herodotus, will be struck with the appearance of those euphonious names, and he will also be struck by the fact that they never appear afterward.

After the election of a speaker, the members went up to be sworn; and now there was a row with the Louisiana Delegation. Stevens objected to the Louisiana Delegation, and Brooks came forward, prompt as ever, to vindicate the cause of innocence and justice. He said that he hoped the House would go on in the ordinary way, and swear in every man, woman, and child that applied for admission. It was hard work to stand, and he thought the gentlemen from Louisiana should have seats. If, after admitting them and paying their mileage, it should be found desirable to get rid of them, they could be kicked out or put out in any manner the House should determine. He knew nothing of the rights of the members from Louisiana, and he didn't care a damn, so long as they were good Confederates and would vote on his side. The country was rich and could afford to pay. These gentlemen had come a long distance for seats, and it would not be in accordance with the rules of chivalry or hospitality to keep them standing, except on one of the standing committees. Memminger could easily print off a few more treasury notes. [Applause by the Louisiana Delegation.]

STEVENS.—These credentials are no credentials at all. Who has ever heard of this pretended Gov. Macpherson ? [Voice—"Read THE ERA."] By what right does he claim that title ? There has been no election in Louisiana, and how was it possible for anybody to get elected ?

Brooks moved that Macpherson's Twenty-second Letter, containing an account of the State election be read for the information of the ignoramus who had just taken his seat. He would there find an official account of the election and its results. But it made no difference

whether there had been an election or not. He put it
upon the ground of courtesy. These gentlemen had
taken a great deal of trouble, and he believed if they
were refused admittance others would be deterred from
asking for seats in the House.

Stevens moved to refer the members from Louisiana
to the committee on credentials.

Allen moved to lay the Delegation on the table.
Lost. Stevens's motion was then carried; the banner of
freedom and truth trailed in the dust; the free-born
citizens of Louisiana were virtually expelled from the
House. From this moment, in my opinion, dates the
visible decline of public virtue in the Confederacy.
What encouragement is there, henceforth, for patriots
ambitious to go to Congress? None! What way is
there left open by which a pennyless Governor like me
can pay his hotel bills, if his friends get nothing to
divide with him? None!

The knees of the Cussed Fool knocked together, and
it was in vain that I strove to administer consolation
and hope to his wounded and bleeding soul. I asked
him to show that the spirit of a man had some place in
him yet, and to resign himself to his fate.

" Resign !" said he, brightening up ; " that is a good
idea. I will resign myself," and immediately he wrote
his resignation as member of Congress, which I accepted
on the spot, and notified the Speaker of the fact in
writing. But that leather-headed ignoramus said the
Cussed Fool was no member at all, and he didn't see
how he could resign a seat which he never possessed.
Therefore, he would not trouble the House with the
matter.

The question then arose how we were to get away from the city without paying our bills. We finally hit upon the expedient of having every thing charged to the Solitary Horseman, who still remains in Richmond waiting at the door of the House patiently, day by day, for the Committee on Credentials to let him in. He hopes by his patient conduct and meek looks, to arouse the pity of the House; and praying that he may succeed, I remain,

Yours, officially,
JAMES B. MACPHERSON.

P. S.—*Jan.* 1*st*, 1864.—This being leap year, sealed proposals for matrimony will be received until the thirty-first day of December next.

J. B. M.

THE END.

www.ingramcontent.com/pod-product-compliance
Lightning Source LLC
Chambersburg PA
CBHW030827020726
47499CB00006B/2100